Praise for Val Griswold-Ford's *Winter Secrets*:

"Griswold-Ford cooks a story as sweet as peppermint cookies in a Christmas stocking. You'll gobble it right up!"

-**Tamara Siler Jones**, author of the
Dubric Byerly Mysteries, Bantam Spectra

A Carter's Cove Advent Story

Winter Storms

VAL GRISWOLD-FORD

ALSO BY VAL GRISWOLD-FORD

Carter's Cove
Winter Secrets
Winter Storms

Available from Dragon Moon Press

The Dark Horseman Trilogy
Not Your Father's Horseman
Dark Moon Seasons
Last Rites

The Complete Guide to Writing Fantasy series (with Tee Morris and Lai Zhao)
Alchemy with Words
The Opus Magnus
The Author's Grimoire

Rum & Runestones (editor)
Spells & Swashbucklers (editor)

Available from Captain's Table Press

Snow (A Dark Horseman Novella)
Convoy (A True Souls Short Story)
Into Thin Air (A Pendragon Casefiles Novella)

Available from ImagineThat! Studios

"The Sun Never Sets" (*A Tale from the Archives short story*)

A Carter's Cove Advent Story

Winter Storms

VAL GRISWOLD-FORD

DARKER
REALITY

DRS

STUDIOS

A **Darker Reality Studios** Novel

Published in the United States of America
by Darker Reality Studios
www.DarkerReality.com

Copyright © 2017 by Val Griswold-Ford
www.VG-Ford.com
and
Darker Reality Studios

Cover design and cover art by Starla Huchton
Designed By Starla (www.DesignedByStarla.com)

Cover layout, interior illustrations, interior layout,
and book design by Scott E. Pond
Scott E. Pond Designs, LLC (www.scottpond.com)

Edited by Sue Baiman
(www.MyEditorIsSue.com)

Library of Congress Cataloging-in-Publication Data
Griswold-Ford, Val
Winter Secrets//Val Griswold-Ford.—1st ed.
p. cm.
1. Fantasy—Fiction

ISBN: 978-1-944672-02-7

PRINTED IN THE UNITED STATES OF AMERICA
10 9 8 7 6 5 4 3 2 1

FIRST EDITION: December 2017

This book is dedicated to KJ, who is the closest thing to a kitchen witch I know.

Acknowledgments

Thank you to everyone who asked for a second Cove book. Thank you to Scott, KJ, Dad, Kris, Lai, Kiaya, and everyone else who supported me through this. Here's to many more Christmases.

- Val Griswold-Ford

Introduction

Welcome back! This is the second book in the Carter's Cove Advent series, which follows the adventures of Molly Barrett, kitchen witch extraordinaire, and her roommate, Schrodinger the CrossCat, during the Christmas season in the magical world of Carter's Cove, Maine. The Cove, for those readers who may not have read the first book (Winter's Secrets), is a town in an alternate but similar dimension to ours that contains not one, but two Gates that allow travelers to come and go from the various Realms in the multi-verse.

This is first and foremost a Christmas story, because Christmas continues to be an important holiday season in my household. In addition to it being a magical time of the year, the traditions of the season have kept my family together, even when things got dark and cold. I think of the Christmas lights on my tree, and how they signify that no matter how harsh the winter, how dark the night, there is always warmth and light, if you know how to look for it. I hope you enjoy your return to the Cove.

Winter Storms

Chapter 1
December 1

"**M**erry Christmas, Aunt Margie!"

Margie Barrett smiled up at the tall young man who had just swept through the front door of her bookstore. "And a very Merry Christmas to you, Drew!" she replied, then lowered her voice, motioning him over to her. "I'm glad you thought of this, honestly. She's been moping around the kitchen for the last week, since the funeral, and it's getting old."

Drew McIntyre sighed, well aware of his girlfriend's current uncharacteristic moodiness. Molly Barrett was normally one of the calmest, cheeriest people he knew--she always had a smile for everyone. But in the past two months, life had reminded all of them how fleeting it could be. Her demeanor had darkened, mirroring the cold, dank nights of late November in Carter's Cove, Maine. It was part of the reason he'd come up with the scheme in the first place.

If it worked, that was.

"I'll do my best," he promised now, grinning at her.

"If anyone can make her smile again, you can," Aunt Margie said. "Oh, and while you're going back there, you can give her this." She handed him a large cardboard box from behind the counter. "This might cheer her up a bit too."

"Tea always does," Drew said, noting the return address on the label. He set off towards the kitchen door, through the small cafe area that graced the bottom floor of CrossWinds Books. Bookcases reached up to the ceiling, making a semi-circle around the six small tables that marked off the tea room. Today, the tables were only half-filled: Stephan and Lucille Dorr shared a table and a pot of tea, she knitting, he reading to her in a low voice; while at another table, Zach Travers was studying for finals, a plate of Molly's sugar cookies half-hidden under a pile of papers, a mug of tea in one hand and a small tablet computer in the other. And, dozing in his large bed by the wood stove in the corner of the room was Schrodinger, right where Drew had hoped he would be.

As if he'd heard the thought (and he probably had, Drew realized), the large CrossCat raised his head. *Drew!* Schrodinger jumped up and bounded over to him. *Did you get it all set up? Is it ready? What's that? Is it part of it?*

"Whoa, whoa, Schrodinger!" Drew laughed, trying not to drop Molly's package or fall over the enthusiastic Cat, who was twining around his feet. Schrodinger was about the size of a large Jack Russell terrier and weighed about 30 pounds, but he was every bit as curious as any house cat Drew had ever known. And that was a dangerous combination, especially in something like a doorway. "Calm down! We're going to--"

CRASH!

Drew landed hard on his shoulder, twisting around as he fell through the doorway to the kitchen so that he didn't flatten either the Cat or the box of tea he was carrying, and managed to smack his head against one of the cabinets against the wall. Schrodinger was smart enough not to get squished, but the tea box didn't fare quite as well. It flew out of Drew's hands as he went down, slamming into the island in the middle of the kitchen with a loud bang.

"What was that?" Molly's voice floated out from the pantry at the back of the kitchen.

Drew shook the cotton from his head as she came out of the small room, her hands full of trays, cups, and plates. Her hazel eyes widened as she saw him there, and she quickly shoved everything onto the island, running over to him.

"Good lord, Drew, what happened?" she demanded, laying a cool hand on his forehead.

"Schrodinger," he replied, and then laughed as she turned to the CrossCat. Schrodinger was crouched down just outside the doorway in the tea room, his tail down and his ears flattened in shame. Beyond him, Drew could see the Dorrs and Zach looking over towards them, and he waved them off. "No, Molly, it's okay. He just got excited."

"What else is new?" Molly said, but her tone was resignedly amused, and she extended a hand to help him get up. Drew took the hand and pressed it to his lips before he clambered to his feet, loving the slight flush the gesture brought to her pale cheeks. Even after a year together, she still blushed every time he kissed her hand. It was charming. And he couldn't stop himself from doing it.

Once again, Phoebe was right, he thought, blessing his grandmother and her seemingly endless courtesy lessons. *I should have known better than to doubt her.*

After he was back on his feet, Drew kept a hold of her hand, drawing her in close for a real kiss. Molly melted against him, her lips warm and tasting faintly of peppermint, vanilla, and sugar.

"You're baking candy cane cookies," he murmured, as they came up for air, and then grinned as she blinked at him.

"How did you know?"

"I can taste them," he said.

Molly blushed again and licked her lips self-consciously. "I was crushing candy canes earlier for the dough."

Drew laughed and snagged one more kiss before letting her

go. He went over to the island and picked up the package. "I think it's okay."

"I was afraid it was something breakable," Molly said, accepting the box from him. Other than one crushed corner where it had hit the island, it was undamaged. She split the tape on the top with a pair of scissors from the knife block, and then turned to look at Schrodinger, who had hopped up onto one of the bar stools that were around the island. "You are lucky," she said severely. "This just happens to contain the new Earl Grey I ordered for you, since you are almost out. As well as my Christmas tea. If it had been damaged..." She left the words hanging, but Drew saw the twinkle in her eyes.

Schrodinger dropped his head. *I didn't mean to,* he said, his mental voice soft. *Please don't tell Santa!*

"It was an accident," Drew assured him. "Santa understands accidents."

He does?

"Of course he does," Molly said, relenting and giving Schrodinger's tufted ears a rub. "Otherwise, Lily and Jack would never get anything. Don't worry - if they haven't gotten on his bad list yet, you haven't either."

The CrossCat perked back up at that, and he leaned over to look into the box, his green eyes bright. *That's a lot of tea! What else did you get?*

Molly tilted the box towards him, showing him an array of little tins, all painted in bright colors. "All sorts of tea," she said. "This cold season has had people going through my supply at a frightening rate. I was afraid I was going to run out before this came in."

"You could go to the grocery store and get tea, you know," Drew said, winking at Schrodinger as Molly took the box of tea into the pantry to put it away.

"You could drink dishwater too, but why would you want

to?" she retorted over her shoulder, and he laughed. Molly's dislike of supermarket tea, which she had once termed "stale, bland packets of tea-colored mush," was legendary.

While she was in the pantry, Drew leaned over to Schrodinger and whispered, "It's all set."

Really? The CrossCat's voice was equally soft.

Drew nodded. "Promise me that you'll remember what her face looks like when she sees it, since I won't be there."

I wish you didn't have to go.

"Me too, buddy." Drew stroked Schrodinger's velvety back, enjoying the rumble of his purr. "Me too. But it's only for a couple of days, and then we'll have the entire rest of December to celebrate together."

Molly came out of the pantry carrying a bag of crushed candy canes, and gave them a suspicious look. "I heard whispering. What are you two hooligans up to now?"

"Hooligans?" Drew said, as Schrodinger pulled himself upright on the stool, both of them blinking innocently. He turned to the CrossCat. "Are we hooligans?"

Only when we watch soccer, Schrodinger said.

"Well, okay, yes. Then we are hooligans," Drew agreed. "But not normally."

No.

Molly shook her head. "I know you two are up to something," she said, setting the bag on the counter with her other cookie ingredients. "But right now, I don't have time to figure it out. I've got cookies to bake."

Drew heaved a sigh. "And I have a Gate to repair." He eyed her hopefully. "Can I get a kiss and a travel cup of tea for the road?"

He walked out of the bookstore five minutes later with more than that--a package of Molly's sweet cranberry scones in his pocket, the taste of candy canes on his lips, and the image of her reaction to the surprised he'd left her in the apartment in his mind.

It almost made up for the fact that he was heading to another Realm for two days without her.

Almost.

✳✳✳

"Are you sure you don't want a ride home tonight? It's snowing again," Aunt Margie said, as they closed up the bookstore that night.

Molly shook her head, strands of her dark hair escaping from underneath her woolen cap. "It's not that cold out, and the walk lets me decompress," she said. "Besides, Schrodinger is with me."

Indeed, he said, sitting next to her and looking very jaunty in his black knit scarf, the black tips of his pointed ears swiveling to catch every sound. *And I'll protect her.*

"From every single snowflake," Molly agreed, chuckling. "Come on, this is the Cove. It's less than fifteen minutes away. We're fine. Go home and tell Uncle Art we said hi."

Molly and Schrodinger waited until Aunt Margie climbed into her little green car, festively adorned with an evergreen wreath on its grill, and drove off. Then the two of them set off through the snow towards their own home.

The night was crisp and cold, but not too cold--the kind of night that seemed to have glass shard edges, a snap in the air that made breathing a bracing exercise. Snowflakes danced lightly around them as they walked, a shower of silvery glitters in the colored lights cast from Christmas decorations in the windows. Snow crunched under her boots.

Schrodinger, of course, glided along silent as a ghost, barely seeming to disturb the air as he paced beside her. From the town center came the sounds of humans--it was Saturday night, after all, so Carter's Cove hadn't quite shut down yet. But Molly's road was quiet, lit by street lamps and more Christmas lights, and the world around her seemed to have settled in for a winter snooze.

Molly's thoughts turned, as they often had during the last two weeks, to Gay Alward. She wondered again if the woman had anyone staying with her. There had been plenty of folks Molly hadn't recognized at the funeral for Tom Alward Sr the week before, but she didn't know if any of them had stayed on. And she hadn't seem Tom Jr, the Alwards' only child, since the funeral.

I hope he's with his mother, she thought, stuffing her hands in her pockets. *If not...*

Everyone grieves in their own way, Schrodinger said softly. *Perhaps he just needs some time alone. And maybe he's there, but hasn't gone out. That happens.*

Maybe. Molly privately thought that the Gate tech was probably just as happy now that his father was gone. Tom Jr and Tom Sr had had some epic public fights over the younger man's decisions recently, including his abrupt departure from the Realms Gate Academy. Drew had told her how much the elder Alward had denigrated and belittled his son every chance he got at the Station. Molly still couldn't believe some of it.

She remember the kindly man who had taken her, Tom, and the rest of their friends camping and fishing on the Elizabeth River when they were younger. The grandfatherly figure who had helped her learn to ride her bike when her father had been called away one summer. The man who had stopped in the bookstore with packages of tea that he'd picked up on his travels.

But people change, and perhaps she'd only seen the public side of his personality. Still, it didn't seem right that Tom Jr wasn't with his mother.

You can't make that decision for him, she reminded herself. *He's a grown man, and he's not your boyfriend. But perhaps it's time to bring another meal over to Gay, and give her some company.*

I think she'd like that, Schrodinger agreed.

They stopped to grab their mail from the box out in front of their brownstone, then trudged inside and up the steps to the second floor landing.

A small wreath was hanging on their door, adorned with small red apples and a brilliant silver bow. Molly smiled. "Drew must have hung it after we left for work this morning," she said, and then sighed, as that reminded her that he wasn't going to be there for at least the next two days.

Schrodinger butted his head into her calf and then stretched up, putting his damp paws on her thigh to get her attention. *Maybe he'll be back sooner,* he said. *It might be an easy fix.*

"It could be," Molly agreed. "We'll hope so."

Unlocking the front door, Molly dropped her keys into the small basket on the shelf next to the door. As she walked into the dining area, she glanced at the mail in her hand: a card from a friend in Boston, fliers, and catalogs, mostly junk mail. She was almost into the kitchen when she finally looked up at the small table tucked under her front window.

Do you like it? Schrodinger asked anxiously, as she stood rooted to the ground in shock. *Please tell me you like it. Drew said you would like it, that it would help make you feel better.*

Molly walked slowly towards the table, almost unable to believe what she was seeing. Instead of the family of snowmen she had set up that morning (and to be honest, it had been hard for her to put them up, as they had been a gift from Gay and Tom Sr a few years ago), there was a three-foot evergreen Christmas tree, its burlap-swaddled roots dressed with a red velvet tree skirt. Multicolored lights twinkled at her, but other than that, the tree was undecorated. In front of it was a familiar red envelope and a little green and silver beaded ornament.

She picked up the envelope and opened it. The card, in Drew's elegant calligraphy, said, "I'm sorry I can't be here to see your face when you find this, but Schrodinger has promised me he'll tell me everything. I know things have been rough these last few months, and I wanted to bring back the sparkle to your eyes, especially for Christmas. But I didn't want to do the same thing we did last year. So here's something different - a new ornament for our first tree together. I hope you like it, and I'll see you in a few days. I love you. Drew."

Molly?

She put down the card and picked up the ornament. It was tiny, the size of a ping-pong ball, and had an intricate netting woven around it of silver and green seed beads. Someone had put a lot of love into making this ornament.

Molly? Schrodinger put one paw on her leg. *Are you okay? Drew said you'd be okay, but now I'm not sure. Are you okay?*

After she'd placed the ornament on the tree, Molly knelt down and hugged him. "Yes," she said. "Yes, I'm okay. It's lovely."

Then why are you crying?

She didn't answer, but just hugged him again and dried her tears on his soft fur.

✳✳✳

The Snow Queen darkened her scrying mirror and turned away, tears of her own glimmering in her green eyes. *It's not my fault, Molly,* she thought, looking out of her window, where snow fell through the dark evergreen trees that surrounded her castle. *I'm so sorry that it's come to this, but this is the only way to save Carter's Cove.*

The tears fell then, hiding the snow from her, but nothing could hide the memories in her mind, or the thundering voice that still rang in her ears.

"They have taken their wars to my lands for the last time!" he'd shouted, pointing an accusing finger at her. "Because you wouldn't listen! So you coddled them, and I have to clean up their traps and their destruction! I won't have it! I'll see how THEY like it!"

"You can't prove it was Carter's Cove, though," she'd

protested.

"It doesn't matter! They're here, and they're just as good a warning as any other place! Better, in fact, because they know you protect them." He had towered over her, dark and threatening. "I want them to realize that I will not let them rampage unchecked over the Known Realms any longer; and that not even you can stop me."

"I can, you know," she'd said. "Don't push me to that."

"You won't, though," he'd sneered. "You've gotten as soft as they have. You should live there."

"You know that's not possible," the Snow Queen had said, stung. "But if it were, I would be proud to live there. Carter's Cove is a good place, with good people. You should not condemn them over the actions of others, especially when you don't know who set the traps in the first place."

"Does it matter?"

"It used to, especially to you."

And that had been the point at which she'd realized how much he'd changed. Something had happened when he'd gone off on one of his travels: a darkness had invaded him, enveloped him. But there was still one thing that hadn't changed.

"Let me prove their goodness to you," she'd said, and he'd paused. "A wager."

"And if I win?"

"I will not stop you from destroying the Cove." The words had felt bitter in her mouth, like poison. "But if I win, you leave the Cove alone."

He had considered that, and then a slow, malicious smile had wreathed his face. "Done."

And now that the die had been cast, the pieces moved into place, all she could do was hope she'd put her trust in the right person.

Chapter 2
December 2

"Saint Michael's Church, Father Christopher speaking."

The priest's deep voice rumbled through the cell phone, easily heard, even over the occasional static. Drew smiled. "Hello, Father. Did you get my package?"

"Drew! Yes, Luke dropped it off earlier this morning. The ornament is lovely. Where did you find them?"

In the background, Drew could faintly hear the sounds of an organ and someone singing. He must have called during choir practice, which meant it was already late afternoon in the Cove. Gauging time while he was repairing Gates in other realms was an irritation he could have done without.

"I went and talked with Catherine Taylor at the Tin Shop to see if she could suggest something for an Advent calendar for Molly," Drew said, leaning back against his pillows. It was late morning where he was, and he had decided to make this call from the cabin he was sharing with the other two techs. "She suggested this new artist she'd found--an old woman who did these beautiful little beaded bottles. I went to her studio outside of Portland, meaning to ask how much the bottles were, and she was working on this amazing little ornament. I knew that's what I wanted as soon as I saw it."

"If they all look like this one, that tree is going to be spectacular," Father Christopher agreed. "And I love the fact that you bought a real tree for her. I already have a spot picked out in back of the church for it."

"Thank you." Drew looked out the window above his head. Late morning sunshine painted the edges of the trees in deep orange and gold. "I know Tom's death hit her hard, and I wanted to remind her just how much I love her."

"You're a good man, Drew." The priest's voice softened. "When are you coming home?"

Not soon enough. "We're scheduled to be done tomorrow afternoon, local time," he said. "That's the only reason I agreed to do this. Mal promised me the rest of the month off, and I'm looking forward to spending it with Molly and Schrodinger."

Father Christopher was smart enough to catch the doubt in his voice. "Are you concerned about meeting that schedule?"

"Not yet." Drew got up and wound his way through the piles of equipment, clothing, and coolers. They'd just dumped their gear yesterday once they'd gotten to the broken Gate. As he walked outside he noticed that the air was cold, but not as cold as Carter's Cove had been when they left. The dirt on the ground was still damp with morning dew but the frost was melting. The sky was a deep, clear blue, with the large orange sun (bigger than Earth's sun) hovering over the tops of the trees. Drew inhaled. No taste of rain or snow.

"The forecast looks good," he said. "If the Gate repairs go as quickly as I hope, and the weather cooperates, we might be done in time to be home tomorrow morning Cove time."

"I'll pray you have no issues," Father Christopher said.

"I'll take all the prayers I can get," Drew said.

After he hung up, Drew went back into the cabin, grabbed a sandwich from the cooler (made on one of Molly's rolls, of course) wondering again how anyone in the Cove would survive if Molly ever stopped baking, and took his tablet back down to the ruins of the Gate.

And ruined it was. Mal had had to create a temporary opening on the nearest Road to get them through close to the Gate, since the components had been completely fried. *At least it was only the inner workings,* he thought. He joined the others, who had several of the stones of the Gate opened already, and were pulling out various components, most of which were beyond repair. *We'd be here a week or more if we'd had to build things from the ground up.*

Of course, if we'd had a real Gate engineer here, instead of me, it wouldn't take us even three days, he thought, wishing again that Tom Sr hadn't died. *Enough of that. The sooner I'm done, the sooner I can go home.*

Drew squatted down in the middle of the arch, and started looking at his tablet. Someone had done a thorough job of destroying the Gate. *I wonder why. What happened here?*

✳✴✳

"Molly? Are you in here?"

Oh god, just go away, please, Molly thought, leaning against the counter in the pantry. In theory, she was trying to figure out what to bake next for the tea shop. In actuality, she was trying to gather her brain cells together and push back the headache she'd woken up with. For some reason (and she hoped it wasn't that she was getting sick, since she didn't have time for that), she was out of sorts and cranky. There were already two trays' worth of burnt cookies in the trash, and she was running out of patience with herself.

She heard Aunt Margie come in to the kitchen.

"Molly? Where are you?"

Molly counted to ten before she called out, "I'm in the pantry, Aunt Margie."

"Are you busy?"

No, I'm napping, Molly thought irritably. Actually, the thought of a nap was more appealing than normal, which meant she probably was getting sick. In December. *Just what I need. Maybe it can wait until Drew comes back, and then I can have him take care of me.* That thought cheered her up, and brought to mind an idea.

"I'm getting ingredients for scones," she called back, reaching out for a couple of canisters from the nearby shelf. "I'll be out in a moment."

When she came out of the pantry, she found not only Aunt Margie but Father Christopher waiting for her. Molly set the canisters down.

"Tea?" she asked, already reaching back to turn on the burner under her favorite kettle. Over the summer, Aunt Margie had offered to install a hot water tap, but Molly had vetoed that idea. Her battered copper kettle had been inherited from her grandmother and it was big enough to fill over twenty tea cups in at a time.

"I won't say no," Father Christopher said, smiling his gentle smile. He took a seat at the island, setting his leather messenger bag on the floor at his feet. "I heard a rumor you got in some new tea yesterday."

"I did indeed." Molly smiled back, unable to resist the priest's charm. She looked at her aunt. "Would you like a fresh cup too?"

"Tea sounds lovely, even though I left my cup upstairs." Aunt Margie sank down onto another stool with a sigh. "Is it really only December second? I'll never last the season."

"You say that every year," Father Christopher said, as Molly got two more mugs.

Her own personal mug was still on the island, damp from her last cup of tea. She pulled out the new tea tins and set them by the mugs, then went to the kitchen door and looked out to see where Schrodinger was.

The CrossCat was asleep in his bed by the wood stove, curled up with his current favorite toy, a stuffed pirate turtle with a patch over one eye. Drew had given him the turtle when he'd come back from his last assignment. It had promptly been named Scurvy, and Schrodinger had insisted it live at the tea shop. Molly contemplated waking him up, but then decided he looked too comfortable to disturb.

"Not going to wake him?" Aunt Margie asked when she rejoined them.

"No. He got far too wound up chasing Lily and Jack around earlier." Molly looked at Father Christopher. "So, Father, to what do I owe this visit? Besides the fact that you heard I had new tea in."

"What, that's not enough?" The priest gave her a look of innocent astonishment that she didn't believe for an instant.

"Not really, no." The kettle started to whistle and Molly pulled it off the burner, pouring hot water into each mug. Then she pulled out new tea bags of her favorite Christmas tea and set them to steep in front of her. "So what are you two up to?"

"I'm just here for the tea, and a chance to be off my feet for a few minutes," Aunt Margie told her. "Well, and to make sure you're feeling all right."

"I'm tired but I'll live," Molly said, then looked at Father Christopher again, one eyebrow raised.

"You know, I used to not have to be interrogated when I came in here," he said.

She just raised the other eyebrow.

"Fine, fine." He reached down and opened the messenger bag. Her eyes widened at the large flat package he pulled out. "As you suspected, I also have something for you from Drew."

"Considering you were in on the scheme last year, I think my suspicions are entirely justified," Molly retorted, taking the wrapped gift from him. It was lighter than she'd expected.

The Christmas ornament on the front of the package was purple, with tiny gold beads at the junctions. It matched the gold and purple fleur-de-lys shimmery wrapping paper. The red envelope attached to the gold ribbon looked a little wan against the shine.

The card inside read, "You've gotten so sad, but music can always make you smile. Will you go singing with us? Drew and Schrodinger"

Molly set the card and the ornament aside, then carefully unwrapped the package. Inside was a slender book of Christmas carols. She blinked, a bit confused.

"Well, well, well, now you three have no excuse not to come out to the church next Thursday night," Father Christopher said, a twinkle in his blue eyes.

"What's next Thursday night?" Molly asked.

"We're doing our first community carol sing," he said. "Eight P.M."

"I don't sing well," she warned him.

"Me either," Father Christopher admitted. "But that's never stopped me."

$*$❋$*$

He stood at the edge of the clearing, hidden in the shadows of the towering pine trees, watching the men work on one side of the stone circle. *Never really understood why they keep the circle, if they're using their precious technology,* he thought irritably.

Because they still honor the old ways, perhaps? Her light mental voice usually soothed him. Today, it was just another irritant.

They have no memory of the old ways, he retorted. *Except how to kill each other and exploit the lands around them.*

You don't know that.

I do. He ground his teeth together. *I do. You know I do.*

She didn't answer, and he watched as the tall blond man, the one who seemed to be in charge, stood in the center of the archway that filled the circle, his arms extended above his head, fingers splayed. If he'd cared to, the watcher could have seen the tendrils of magic snaking out from the man's fingertips, connecting him to the mechanisms inside the arch. The Gates the humans constructed now were a mix of technology and magic, requiring their engineers and technicians to be magically attuned to the Roads that connected the various Realms.

A low hum filled the air as the other two men laid their hands on the sides of the arch, obviously adding Power to the Gate circuits. The blond man in the middle continued to move his fingers as if playing an invisible stringed instrument, tugging and guiding various magical threads to manipulate the innards of the Gate.

The hum changed tone as he worked, and the watcher grudgingly admired his artistry. This was someone who actually seemed to understand the delicate balance of magic within a Gate, who saw it as a living thing, not just a bunch of circuitry to be used. It was humans like this that he would actually miss.

You don't have to miss them, you know. Her voice was back. *You could just stop this now, walk away, and let life go on.*

No, I can't. You know that. His lips thinned, and he tamped down the memories her comment brought. *This has to stop. I can't let them do this any more.*

Not yet. You promised me.

He grunted, already regretting that he'd let her talk him into giving them one last chance. The more time he gave them, the more opportunity they had to ruin other realms.

But he had promised her. One last chance. He looked down at the Gate again. *They will let you down, you know. They always do. Even him.*

Not this one. There was actually a hint of humor in her voice. *You're going to lose this bet, Old Man.*

We'll see.

Chapter 3
December 3

"Anybody got a cup of tea for a lonely, cold, parched soul?"

Schrodinger's ears perked up as the sound of Lai Zhao's voice floated through the quiet bookstore. It was still early enough in the Christmas season that folks were going home after work instead of trying to shop. And really, for the first two weeks of December, the only people who came in after six P.M. were the diehards and the high school students looking to get some project work done in a quiet place.

The CrossCat had been drowsing in his bed next to the wood stove, half-listening to the three girls at the table in front of him discussing their papers on the role of the Sea Roads in the development of Carter's Cove before and after World War II. Now, however, he hopped up, stretched, and then trotted over to the tall Asian girl who was shaking snowflakes from her long, dark hair.

Lai! He rubbed his cheek against her knee-high leather boots, feeling the cold from outside sink through his fur. *Is it snowing again?*

"I don't think it ever stopped," Lai told him, crouching down to rub his ears. "How's Molly doing today?"

Better. She's excited, and she got more sleep last night than she did before, so she's feeling better. Drew's coming home tonight, you know.

She has a special meal planned for him.

"I hope it's okay if it sits for a while," Lai said, grinning and winking at him. "I think she might be distracted." She stood up and picked up the leather messenger bag she'd put on the floor. "Come on!"

Schrodinger followed her into the kitchen, reflecting that it was fun to be in on Christmas secrets. Molly was singing along with Bing Crosby on the radio as she rolled out pastry dough. The entire store smelled of apples, spices, and caramel, which meant she was making more of her turnovers. She'd debuted them during the fall season to great acclaim. In fact, they'd edged out her cinnamon rolls as the most popular thing on the menu for a bit. And that was almost unheard of in Carter's Cove, where a batch of Molly's cinnamon rolls was usually gone before the icing finished setting.

"It smells divine in here," Lai said, shedding her stylish wool coat and sinking onto a stool. "And warm. God, I thought I wouldn't warm up again, and that was just walking from my office to the car."

"It could be worse," Molly said, putting her rolling pin aside. "If it wasn't snowing, it would be colder. But I have something that can help."

She turned, grabbed a heavy earthenware mug and filled it, not with hot water, but with hot apple cider from a pot she had simmer on the stove. Then she dropped a chai tea bag into the mug. Handing it to Lai, she said, "Try this."

Lai shuddered dramatically as she accepted the drink. "Ugh, I still don't know how I survive every winter."

"Because you were born here, like the rest of us, and don't know any different?" Molly chuckled as she put a plate with two turnovers on it in front of her friend. The small triangles of sweet dough were golden brown, drizzled with caramel and bulging with apples, spices, raisins, and more of Molly's homemade caramel sauce. "Watch out, those just came out of the oven. They're very hot."

Besides, you'd miss us too much if you went away, Schrodinger added, jumping up on the other stool. He looked mournfully at Molly, who shook her head but put a large latte mug full of his favorite Earl Grey in front of him. Schrodinger took his tea exactly like the hero of his favorite Star Trek TV series--hot and black.

"True." Lai bit into one of the turnovers and moaned, half in pleasure, half in pain.

"I told you they were hot!" Molly said.

"They taste better hot," Lai mumbled, trying to suck air into her burned mouth and chew at the same time.

Molly shook her head. "How can you taste anything with scorched taste buds?"

"Bah, caramel can't scorch my taste buds," Lai said, still fanning her mouth. "They've been fire-tested with wasabi. The roof of my mouth might never be the same, though."

Schrodinger dipped his tongue delicately into his tea, trying hard to control his excitement. Then he snuck a look at the clock. Quarter to seven. Almost time for Aunt Margie to come over the store's intercom and announce that they would be closing in ten minutes. Then they could get on to the real fun--once Lai convinced Molly to leave the kitchen with her, that was.

"So, Miss Molly, I hear you have a hot date planned for tonight," Lai said casually, taking a sip of her chai cider.

"That's the rumor," Molly said, turning back to her dough so Lai couldn't see her blush. Schrodinger saw it, though, and he bet Lai did too. "Drew texted this morning and said they'd be home tonight. I thought, since it's so cold, I'd make a beef stew."

"Do you know when he's coming?" Lai asked, all innocence, but Schrodinger hastily took another drink of tea so he wouldn't snort and give it all away. Lai was clever, she was. Molly wasn't even aware she was being led.

Still rolling out the dough, Molly shook her head. "He just said this evening, so I left the stew in the crock-pot. There are biscuits in the fridge that just need to be warmed up as well."

"He's a lucky man," Lai said. She took another bite of her turnover (a smaller one, Schrodinger noticed) and then said, "How will you know when he's back?"

"He's supposed to text when he comes through the Gate." Molly put her rolling pin in the sink and took a pizza cutter from the counter next to her. The large rectangle of dough rapidly became smaller squares; Molly filled one corner of each little square with her special mixture. Caramel from a pot on the stove joined the apples, spices, and raisins on the dough, and then she folded the opposite corner down, creating triangular packages. She pressed the edges together with a fork to seal them, then transferred the turnovers to a baking sheet next to her before putting the entire thing in the oven and removing the sheet that had been there before.

Schrodinger loved to watch Molly in the kitchen. When she was "in the zone," as she called it, it was an intricate dance that she performed, taking the most mundane of ingredients and transforming them into amazing goodies. She said it was just cooking, but Schrodinger knew it was more than that. Molly was magic in the kitchen, never working from actual recipes unless she was redacting them. In her hands, food became something more than it normally was. She always knew what went with what, and the only time she burnt things was when she was feeling cross. The smell of smoke was usually a sign to avoid her.

Now, he and Lai watched as Molly took a bit of the caramel and mixed it with some of her homemade icing, thinning it with just a bit of apple cider so it would drizzle nicely over the warm turnovers. Her spoon moved expertly, laying down thin lines of icing perfectly across each golden pastry. Then she moved the tray of finished turnovers to the far counter, where they joined the rest of their fellows and continued to cool.

Just as she came back to the island to join them, the intercom crackled and Aunt Margie's voice said, "Attention, folks. We're closing in ten minutes. Please bring your final purchases to the checkout counter downstairs, and we'll see you tomorrow."

Molly sat down on the third stool and picked up her own mug of chai cider. "The last tray should only take about fifteen minutes," she told Schrodinger. "So we'll be out of here on time, and will have plenty of time to meet Drew at home."

Okay, he said. He knew better, but he wasn't going to spoil anything, and it wasn't his night, anyways. This one required Lai. Or rather, Lai's car, since Molly didn't have one.

"Can I help?" Lai asked. "Then you can get out earlier. I can even give you a ride home."

"Sure, although there's not much to do," Molly said. "I did most of the dishes and set everything out for tomorrow already, so DC can fill any tea orders. Mostly all I need to do is sweep the kitchen and the tea room, bank the fire in the wood stove, finish off the last batch of turnovers, and make sure they're all put away." She considered for a moment. "If you can sweep the tea room once the door is locked, Lai, I can finish up in here."

They chatted and sipped their hot beverages while the turnovers baked. Then, as Molly cleaned up in the kitchen, Lai and Schrodinger tidied up the tea room, wiping down tables and sweeping the floor. Molly joined them as they were finishing and she knelt down in front of the wood stove, carefully banking the fire for the night. All DC or Sonya (the other clerk Aunt Margie had hired) would have to do in the morning was breathe some life into the coals and add wood.

"Molly, do you need a ride home?" Aunt Margie asked, coming into the kitchen, already clad in her heavy lumberjack coat and the hat Molly's mother had knit for her. "It's too cold for the two of you to be walking home."

"Lai's taking us home," Molly said, and Lai nodded. "We're fine, Aunt Margie."

"Good." Aunt Margie shooed them all out the door and locked it behind her. "Enjoy your day off!" she called, as she strode off to her car.

We will! Schrodinger called back, already bounding towards Lai's car. In keeping with her view on life, Lai had eschewed the little black sports car her mother had wanted to buy her in favor of a sleek Land Rover, customized to fit the unique environments she took it into as a surveyor.

Schrodinger jumped into the back seat, barely able to contain his glee. *Now?*

"Yes," Lai said, waiting until Molly had her seat belt fastened before she steered the Rover out of its parking spot. "We're ready."

"Wait, Lai, this isn't the way to my apartment," Molly said, as they passed her corner and continued on.

"I know." Lai grinned at her. "Open the glove box."

Molly gave her a suspicious look, but opened the glove compartment and pulled out a fragrant evergreen branch. Attached to the middle of the little bough was a gold beaded ornament; still in the glove box was the familiar red envelope.

"You're rotten!" Molly cried, but Schrodinger heard the joy in her voice. Just a little bit, but more than he'd heard in the last few weeks, and it made his heart swell. "You tricked me!"

Lai chuckled. "You don't know the half of it. Open the envelope."

"Molly, I know we had plans for this season, and it starts tonight. Help us find the perfect tree? Love, Drew and Schrodinger." Molly turned to Schrodinger. "How did you keep this a secret from me?"

CrossCats keep excellent secrets, he said smugly. *Are you happy?*

"Very," she said, rubbing his head. "And I'll bet Drew is meeting us there, isn't he?"

You'll see.

✳✳✳

Molly, Lai, and Schrodinger piled out of the car at Lavalle's Christmas Tree Farm and wove their way through the crowds heading into the lots, looking for the perfect Christmas tree. As they entered the farm itself, Molly kept one hand in her pocket, cradling her cell phone, waiting for the text message she knew would come.

But as the minutes stretched on and on, her faith began to flag. And then doubts started to creep in. Not that he'd dumped her; no, Drew wouldn't do that, not even if he was ready for the relationship to be over, which he hadn't shown any inclination of. No, but what if the Gate repairs had been delayed? Mal would have called her, right? To tell her? She started to pull the phone out to see if she had any messages, although she hadn't felt it vibrate.

Oh, oh, oh! Molly, Lai, come on! Come here!

Her heart swelled. It had to be Drew. It had to be. Molly broke into a run, nearly slipping and falling on the snow.

She and Lai burst into the clearing at about the same time, but there was no Drew there. Just Schrodinger, dancing enthusiastically around what Molly had to admit was the perfect tree.

I found it! He shouted, shaking his head. *And it even has a bird's nest in it!*

Swallowing her disappointment, Molly smiled at him and knelt to tie their tag to the base of the tree. Last year, her father had told Schrodinger that the best, most lucky Christmas trees had a leftover bird's nest in them, and that finding a tree with one in it meant good luck for the coming year.

"You're right," she told him, sitting back on her heels after she finished tying their tag on. "It's perfect."

It was--a small Balsam fir, fragrant and full, just a bit taller than her. And the precious bird's nest sat about three quarters of the way up, fully intact. Lai reached up and took the nest out carefully.

We can put candy in it, right? And put it back in the tree once we decorate it? Schrodinger asked, looking at Molly.

"Of course," she said, forcing cheerfulness into her voice. "That would be really neat."

She couldn't fool him, though. Schrodinger put one wet paw on her leg and said, *He'll be back. It's just a delay. We can call the Station and confirm it.*

"I know." Molly hugged him, heedless of the snow melting in his fur. It had started to snow again while they walked through the trees: a fine, light snow, like the kiss of frozen stars. "We'll call Mal when we get home if Drew's not there."

It was a quiet ride back. Lai dropped them off at the front and waited until Molly had unlocked the door before driving off into the snow, waving.

She'd been hoping that maybe Drew had come straight to the apartment from the Station--it might have been a rougher trip than he'd anticipated, she reasoned, and he might have just come back, gone to shower, and fallen asleep before he remembered to text or meet them. He did have a key, after all.

But the apartment was dark and quiet, the lights on the tiny Christmas tree on her table the only illumination. Schrodinger looked up at her as she turned on the lights in the kitchen.

I'll check the bedroom, he said, trotting off.

Molly watched him go, knowing he would find the bedroom just as empty as the rest of the apartment. Drew's jacket and boots weren't in the foyer.

He hadn't come back.

She called the Station while Schrodinger watched her with worried eyes. "Hi Luke," she said, when the Gate tech came on the line. "Are Drew and the others back yet?"

There was a slight hesitation before he answered, so slight that she almost missed it. "No, he's not back yet," he said. "We're expecting him at any minute though. There's a Road storm that blew up out of nowhere, and it caused some...fluctuations."

Ice crept along her veins. "Fluctuations? What do you mean?"

"It's nothing serious, Molly," Luke hastened to assure her. "The Gate blinked a couple of times, and then we lost the connection. We can't get it back until the storm blows through. But no one was on the Road between the two Gates when the connection went down. I promise you."

Molly swallowed. "And Drew and the others are stuck at the other end?"

"Only Drew, actually," Luke admitted. "Steve and Gus had just come through when the connection was severed, and they said he was still at the cabin, that he sent them on ahead."

"What?" she whispered.

"We're monitoring the situation now, and as soon as we can get the Gate connection back, we will," Luke said. "I promise you, Molly, we're doing everything we can to get Drew back home, but with that storm, we can't even open a temporary Gate. Right now, he's probably in the staff cabin, trying to call home. The phones won't work until the Gate reopens." He paused as someone spoke to him in the background. "Mal says the storm is supposed to blow over within the next few hours, so I'm sure we'll have him home by morning."

The reassurances rang hollow in her ears, but Molly thanked him and hung up the phone. Something was wrong. Something was terribly wrong, and there wasn't a damn thing she could do.

Schrodinger came up to her. *What did they say? Where's Drew?*

"Still at the Gate, apparently," Molly said, and told the CrossCat what Luke had said.

Do you want me to go and look for him? Schrodinger asked her, laying his head against her leg.

For one long moment, Molly considered it, but then she shook her head. "No, if there's a Road storm that knocked the connection loose, then I'd be worrying about both of you, and that would drive me nuts. Luke is right. Drew is probably frantic trying to call from the staff cabin there. The storm can't last that long. They'll get the Gates reconnected and then he'll come home."

If you say so, Schrodinger said, but his tone indicated that he didn't believe it.

Neither did she.

✳✷✳

Drew eyed the sky as he, Steve, and Gus packed up the rest of the equipment onto the sled they'd brought with them. The sun was still high, but there were clouds coming in. The Gate Station at Carter's Cove had warned them about a snow storm growing south of the Gate they were working on, and he wanted to be long gone before it got to them.

"We all set, guys?" he called, and Steve nodded.

"Good to go," he said, the southern drawl sounding remarkably out of place in the wintry setting. He'd come up from one of the Gate Stations in Austin to help Carter's Cove over the season, and his accent had most of the girls in town swooning. The fact that he was tall, tanned, and (most importantly) not from the Cove was gravy, or so Molly had told Drew.

"Good." Drew spared one more look at the darkening sky. "Then get that through the Gate. I'm going to check the cabin one more time, to make sure the only things we left were what the next crew will need."

Steve nodded. "Want help?"

"Nah, you and Gus go through." Drew looked at the older man standing by the Gate arch, another temporary assistant from one of the Northeast Stations, although he hadn't volunteered which one. Gus had been remarkably reticent, but he had been a good worker. "I'll be right behind you."

"Good enough." Steve started the engine on the sled and began to guide it down to the Gate.

As he turned and headed back up the path to the little cabin that was the way station for the crew, Drew felt the Gate open. Each technician and engineer worked the Gate magics a little differently, but as he hadn't worked with either Steve or Gus for very long, Drew had no idea which one it was. If it had been Luke or Tom, he would have.

Drew grimaced at that thought. He liked Tom, even though the guy had hurt Molly pretty badly, and he'd overheard at least one of the tongue-lashings the younger Alward had gotten from his father before the man had passed away. No one deserved to be talked to like that. He didn't blame Tom for not being around now, but at the same time, the Gate Station needed him.

So does his family, though, he reminded himself, pushing open the door. *Although town gossip has it that he's not there either.*

He did a quick sweep of the interior, coming up with a charging cable (Steve's) and a half-used notebook with row upon row of Gate coordinates and recipes (Gus's, and Drew made a mental note to introduce the man to Molly before he left). He stuck both in his pockets and turned back to the door.

However, he found the door blocked by the huge bulk of a man dressed in grey, silver, and white furs. Snow hung around him like a shroud, and his breath danced in the suddenly frigid air of the cabin. Drew had just enough time to notice all of this, and then pain erupted from the right side of his face and the world went black.

✳✱✳

You didn't have to hit him. Her voice was sharp.

The old man grunted as he heaved the limp body up over his shoulder. "Easiest."

Liar. You could have simply put him to sleep.

"I did. I just used my fist instead of magic." His face twisted into a bit of a satisfied smile, remembering the feeling of his hand hitting the man's head.

What happened to you, Old Man? When did you get this vindictive? You were never cruel before.

Her words stung him a bit. "Perhaps you just never noticed. You were too busy pretending to be human, hoping they'd accept you. They never will, you know." He sneered. "Especially not now."

You underestimate them.

"You trust them too much." He looked up at the sky and scowled. "Go bother someone else, Jade. I'm busy."

Chapter 4
December 4

The world was dark. And painful. And warm.

Drew swam up through inky blackness towards consciousness, feeling every muscle and tendon in his body begin to protest as he came back to the world a piece at a time. The darkness finally resolved itself into his eyelids, and he steeled himself for more pain when he opened his eyes.

At least whoever had kidnapped him had had the decency to give him a room with an actual bed. And he wasn't tied up, he realized. In fact, he was snuggled under a massive down comforter in a bed that could easily fit him, Molly, Schrodinger and about four of their closest friends. It was soft and warm, and Drew had to fight the temptation to just sink back into unconsciousness. The only thing that kept him from doing so was the need to find out what had happened.

He struggled up to a seated position and opened his eyes slowly, his head spinning a bit when he moved. *I hope it's not a concussion*, he thought, touching the spot on his jaw where the giant that had surprised him in the cabin had hit him with a huge fist. Running his hand over the back of his head, Drew found a matching bump where his head had hit the floor and winced. He sat still for a couple of moments, trying to determine if he had any other injuries.

There weren't, he found. Other than the two lumps on his head, he hadn't been harmed. The aches in his body were muscular, probably from being carried from the cabin over the giant's shoulder (he assumed), but there were no cuts, no obvious wounds.

Which means he wants me alive, whoever he is. Drew squinted through the dimness of the room, trying to see if there was anyone else with him. There wasn't. As his eyes adjusted to the subdued lighting, he realized the room was large, a bedroom like one at a luxury hotel. Two large bookcases loomed out of the twilight, bracketing a fireplace that had the dim glow of coals nestled in its heart. There was a desk under what Drew realized was a large window, covered now with curtains that shut out most of the light. And, across the room from him, was a door.

He slipped from the bed stiffly, wondering how long he'd been unconscious. There was a furry feeling to his tongue, as if he'd forgotten to brush his teeth before going to bed, and his reactions were a bit slow. But he was relatively steady on his feet--a good sign. Drew made a beeline for the door, hoping against hope that this was all a mistake, or a bad dream...

It was locked.

Drew leaned his forehead against the cool wood, and cursed under his breath. Of course it was locked. *Whoever took me wants me alive, but out of the way,* he thought. *But why? Why me? I'm just a Gate tech. No one special.*

His mind offered his grandmother's face for a moment, but Drew doubted it. Perhaps if he was still in his hometown, but he wasn't, and there hadn't been anything he'd heard about his grandmother recently anyways.

Then Molly's face appeared. She would be frantic by now, if she wasn't royally pissed at him for not being home. No, Molly wouldn't be pissed, she'd be worried sick. He hoped Lai and Schrodinger had been able to keep her calm.

Gotta get home, Drew thought, pushing himself off the door and turning to look at the room again. There had to be something he could use to get out. *I am NOT missing the entire Christmas season with Molly and Schrodinger. Not an option. There has to be some way to get out of here, get to a Gate, and get home.*

Home. Odd how quickly Carter's Cove had become home to him. It was so different from Marionville, the CrossRoads town in the Midwest where he'd grown up, and yet similar in so many ways. A small, cozy town. The kind of town he'd swore he would never live in again, where everyone knew everyone else, and secrets didn't really exist. When he'd come to the Cove last year, he'd been counting down the days until he could transfer out to one of the big Gate Stations out on the West Coast.

And then he'd met Molly, and Schrodinger, and lost his heart. And his mind, one of his buddies from the Academy had kidded him, but Drew didn't care. He no longer wanted to be an engineer in one of the big Gate Stations. He wanted to stay in Maine, with its lousy weather and odd inhabitants and Yankee proclivities.

He wanted to stay with Molly.

First I have to get back there. And that means figuring out where I am now, he decided, moving towards the window. Yanking the curtains aside, he blinked and ducked his head at the sudden sunlight that shot shards through his aching head. When the pain subsided and he could see again, Drew groaned.

The world was white: ice, and snow, and clear blue sky as far as he could see; tumbling out along and up to the sides of distant mountains. The snowfields were full of ancient pine trees with mantles of white, marching off into the distance. The sun above him (and it was only one sun, close to the size of Earth's sun, which meant he wasn't in the same Realm he'd been in before) sparkled on the snow.

There would be no escape for him this way. The window was locked, and even it he'd been able to break it, it was a second-story room, with no convenient nearby trees. He cursed and banged his hand against the window.

"Funny, that's not usually the reaction my house guests have when they see the view," a light voice said from behind him. Drew whirled around, astonished. He hadn't heard the door open or close.

But he was definitely not alone anymore--and the door was still shut tightly. However, standing in the middle of the room, surrounded by a pale light that seemed to emanate from within her slender form, was the Snow Queen.

Her silver-blonde hair was intricately braided and wrapped around her head, a cushion for her small platinum and diamond crown to rest upon. Drew had only seen her once before, at the Ball last Christmas, dressed in a beautiful gown of icy white and blue, but she was just as impressive in the simple dark green dress she was now wearing. A cape of fur, lightly dusted with snow, lay across her shoulders.

"House guest?" Drew said finally, after he'd gaped at her for a few minutes. The fur she wore reminded him of the furs the giant had worn. "Funny, I don't feel like a house guest at the moment. Maybe it's because house guests aren't usually locked in their rooms."

The Snow Queen looked at him, her lovely face shadowed with either sorrow or regret. He couldn't decide which, but there was steel underneath--that he saw clearly. "I am sorry for that," she said finally. "It was necessary, but only until I could speak with you. It will no longer be locked."

"Was it?" Now Drew was getting annoyed. "Why? What have I done to you?"

"Nothing," she said. "And I'm sorry you have been embroiled in this, Drew, but I had no choice. This was the only way."

"The only way to do what?" he demanded.

Her next words shot an icicle through his heart. "The only

way to save Carter's Cove. And quite possibly, the rest of the humans in the Realms."

✳✱✳

"So, my fine furred feline friend, what shall we do today?"

Molly toyed with the remains of her scrambled eggs and looked over at Schrodinger, who was finishing up his first mug of Earl Grey. They had both slept in, as was their wont on their off days, and had taken a leisurely breakfast as they watched the snow fall. The light snowflakes from the night before had turned into a steady storm, and Molly wondered how many new feet they would end up with before it blew out to sea. It had the feel of a storm that was settling in for a long visit.

The CrossCat sat back on his haunches and brushed a paw over his whiskers, getting the last precious drops of tea from them. *Well, we have to make cookie dough,* he said. *But we need to take a walk too. Up to the Station, to see when Drew is coming back.*

"Yes." Molly nodded. "I'm running low on a few things too, and I want more cranberries for cranberry bread."

She got up and picked up their breakfast dishes. A quick rinse and they went into the dishwasher. "Let me just take a shower and we'll head out."

It took a bit longer than that, of course. They couldn't show up at the Gate Station empty-handed. Molly had learned long ago that the best way for her to get information from Mal and the other Gate personnel was through their stomachs, and she happened to have some amaretto brownies that she'd been saving to make for just such an occasion.

She and Schrodinger walked slowly through the snow, feeling the crisp air against their faces, a fabric shopping bag over her shoulder with the pan of brownies and a tin of her sugar cookies in it. The Gate Station was only a fifteen minute walk from her apartment in the summer, but in the winter, it took them almost half an hour to get to the large mansion on the edge of the town that housed the Land Gate of Carter's Cove.

Once the town had been large enough to merit a full Station (as opposed to just a way station, which is what many towns had), the Gate had been enclosed within a large brick mansion that could not only house it, but also the personnel needed to keep it running smoothly.

Molly and Schrodinger hiked up the long, winding driveway, enjoying the snow sculptures that loomed out of the falling snow around them. The entire Cove decorated for Christmas, but Mal liked to do a theme, and Molly decided this year's was her favorite so far. He'd chosen Christmas Past, and the lawn was dotted with caroling snowmen carrying lit candles (courtesy of a small magical cantrip that kept the flames flickering without melting either the wax or the snowman in question, or going out due to weather), a sleigh with snowmen being pulled by snow reindeer, and other scenes from the Cove's past. In the falling snow, it was like walking through a dream.

The house itself reared up in front of them, decked in green and gold garlands, with thousands of icicle lights hanging from its roof and towers. Molly remembered Drew's groans of pain the night he'd come home after they'd hung the lights. Rather than use magic to hang them, Mal had insisted on ladders. And had then retreated to his office to let the "younger, stronger members of the staff" actually do the work.

The wreath on the front door had glass candy canes and peppermint starlites on it, the decorations almost glowing against the dark evergreen boughs. Molly didn't knock, but opened the door and let Schrodinger bound in ahead of her.

Hi Heidi! Hi Porter! He paused on the mat inside the foyer to shake all the snow from his fur. Then he ran into the main entryway to greet the Station's receptionist.

"Hi Schrodinger!" Heidi replied, putting down her book and

pushing her glasses back up on her nose. She was a dark-haired older woman with twinkling grey eyes, a friendly smile, and a drawer full of treats for the CrossCat and anyone else who visited the Station. On his pillow beside the reception desk, her old tabby cat Porter raised his head and meowed a welcome.

Schrodinger paused by Porter, touching noses in greeting, and then rubbed up against Heidi's leg. *Did you miss me?*

"I always miss you!" Heidi told him, stroking his head. "Porter and I love to have you come by!" She smiled at Molly, who had finished knocking the snow off herself, hung up her coat, and joined them. "Hi Molly!"

"Hi." Molly smiled back at her. "Any news on Drew?"

Heidi's smile faltered a bit, and she shook her head. "Not yet, but don't you worry. Mal and the guys have been working all night trying to bring the Gate there back online. For some reason, it just won't reconnect."

"Have you ever heard of that happening before?" Molly asked.

Heidi and Schrodinger both nodded. *Sometimes the storms on the Roads can change the path of the Road, if they're strong enough,* he said. *And if the path is shifted far enough, the Gate won't have the right coordinates to connect to it anymore.*

"How do you fix that?" Molly said, interested despite her worry.

Build a new Gate, once you determine where the Road has gone, Schrodinger said. *And hope that something connects to the old Gate at some point, so you don't waste the arch. They're not easy to build.*

Molly swallowed at that. "What about the people on the other side of the Gate that doesn't work anymore?"

Schrodinger suddenly seemed to realize what he'd said. *Oh, Molly, there are other ways to get to someone besides a Gate!* He went up to her and rubbed his head against her leg encouragingly. *Not everyone uses the Gates to travel; it's just the easiest way for many to go. If there is a great enough need, the Roads can be manually moved, or a Gate opened. It just takes a lot of energy and magic and talent. Don't worry. Drew isn't lost forever. He'll be back.*

Mal said the same thing when she and Schrodinger went to deliver their goodies to the techs and engineers in the Gate Room.

"Don't worry, Molly," the grizzled older man told her, switching his ever-present cigarette to the other side of his mouth. "We are not leaving anyone there. We'll get the damn Gate open again." He nodded towards the Gate arch, where a group of people with tablet computers, lit candles, and smoking censors were doing various arcane-looking things. "No matter how long it takes, or who we have to drag in to help."

"That's good," Molly said, handing him the wrapped pan of brownies and the tin of sugar cookies. "I'm baking later today, so I'll send up some more supplies. How are you doing for rolls?"

"We can always use more." Mal took the treats and then teased her, "Maybe we'll have to stash the boy someplace to get more treats out of you, eh?" Then he relented when she scowled at him. "I'm kidding, I'm kidding!" He reached out and laid a hand on her arm, his oddly light eyes serious for once. "I am sorry that I had to send him, Molly. I know he had the month off, but with Tom gone and us down an engineer...I had no choice."

"I know," Molly said, turning to look at the Gate again. She wasn't mad at Mal, not really. "He knew. It's his job."

Mal squeezed her arm. "He'll be back soon."

Molly nodded, still watching the group at the Gate, not trusting herself to say more. She heard him sigh and then leave, presumably to put the treats in the kitchen where the others could help themselves, since he didn't cross in front of her.

She realized she didn't recognize most of the people around the Gate. Steve and Luke were both there, but there were at least six more that she hadn't seen before.

The Gate itself dominated the room, which was in what might have been called a solarium in a normal mansion. Overhead, the massive glass roof let filtered light down to play along the curving granite-sheathed arches of the Gate (the second of its kind to stand on that spot) and the grass that carpeted the room. Real grass, not AstroTurf or carpet, keeping the Gate grounded to the land.

Like all the children who had grown up in the town, Molly had learned how Captain James Carter had sailed into the Cove via a Sea Road and the Sea Gate, and discovered the first Land Gate, a simple stone circle around a wooden arch high on the hill. How he had founded the town to take advantage of the two Gates, and fought off invaders who had attempted to take over by destroying those first two Gates. How his sons had rebuilt the Gates and the town, allowing the Cove to grow and become a major hub to the Realms around them. But it had always just been knowledge in the back of her mind.

Funny how important it is now, she thought, watching Steve open one of the panels on the side of the Gate and squint into the innards. *I never thought my life would depend on a Gate opening so much.*

Schrodinger had left her as well, trotting down to the group, his tail waving and his ears swiveling. He was twice as curious as any house cat she'd ever met, and she had no doubt that he was itching to help in any way he could. She knew that the only thing keeping him here at the moment was his promise to her that he wouldn't go off looking for Drew on his own.

However, that won't stop him from offering advice to anyone who will listen, Molly thought, her lips twitching in a smile despite herself.

And true to form, Schrodinger came up next to Steve, peering in with him. The tech nodded.

"They could do worse than listen to him," said an unexpected voice from beside her, and Molly nearly jumped out of her skin. "CrossCats have an innate sensitivity to the paths of the Roads and he might be able to sniff out a new track for them. If the Road truly has shifted."

The scent of vanilla, peppermint, and ice rushed over Molly. She turned to see the Snow Queen standing beside her.

"Do you really think he could help?" she said, since it would have been rude to come out and say what she really wanted to, which was "What the heck are you doing here, how did you get here, and why are you reading my mind?"

The Snow Queen laughed, a remarkably normal-sounding laugh. "Sorry, I didn't mean to. Sometimes I forget that not everyone can hear thoughts like I can. I didn't mean to intrude." She looked at the CrossCat, who had abandoned Steve to sit next to another tech, leaning in to look over her shoulder into the panel that she was poking a long metal tool into. "But yes, he is a valuable resource to them, if they realize it."

They watched the tech turn to Schrodinger, clearly asking him something, although Molly couldn't tell what. Schrodinger cocked his head for a moment, considering, and then nodded.

"I knew they were smart," the Snow Queen said. "Now, Molly, while your little guardian is busy, I would like to speak with you, if I may." She looked around them pointedly. "In private."

"Me?" Molly blinked. "Why me?"

The Snow Queen smiled. "I have something for you."

"You do?"

Linking her arm into Molly's, the Snow Queen said simply, "Yes."

There was little else Molly could do but walk alongside her. Everyone took one look at them and got out of the way as they walked along the grass to the door at the end of the room, back the way Molly and Schrodinger had come in just a few minutes earlier. Heidi looked up in surprise as they entered the foyer, but didn't say anything as the Snow Queen steered Molly into one of the empty receiving rooms.

The front of the mansion had several rooms especially for travelers to rest and recover from their journey before either going off onto the Roads again or down into the Cove. This one had several comfortable chairs grouped around a fireplace, and a small table in the corner of the room that held a machine for making coffee, tea, or hot chocolate from single serve pods, a basket of assorted pods, and a couple of mugs. The Snow Queen pointed to one of the chairs; Molly sank into it, wondering what on earth one of the major personages of the Realms could have for her.

"You look nervous," the Snow Queen said, settling into the chair opposite her, shedding her fur cloak as she did so. Her dark green dress was plain but exquisitely made; there was the slight sparkle of silver shot through the fabric, and Molly could see the faintest patterning of snowflakes on the hem. Her pale hair was braided into a coronet around her temples, holding her diamond tiara in place. Molly felt dowdy next to her radiance.

"Well, it's not every day the Snow Queen shows up and asks for a private chat with me," she said honestly. "I'm not sure what I should be feeling."

The Snow Queen laughed. "I promise, I have nothing but good news for you," she said. "Would it make you feel more comfortable if I asked you to just call me Jade? The Snow Queen is such a formal lady, after all, and I'm not really feeling that formal today."

Molly eyed the tiara. "That's your everyday coronet, then?"

Jade laughed again, and waved her hand. The tiara disappeared. "Is that better?"

Molly opened her mouth, thought better of it, and then shook her head, confused. "I...yes, yes, it is, I guess," she said finally. "How can I help you?"

Jade smiled. "First, you can relax. I have some good news for you. I've just come from talking to Drew, and he sends his love."

That was NOT what Molly was expecting to hear. She shot to her feet. "Drew? Where is he? Is he okay?"

"He's fine, Molly," Jade said, pulling her back down. Molly sat, unable to believe what she was hearing. "He sends his love to you."

"His love." Molly looked at her. "When is he coming back?"

To her surprise, Jade dropped her head. "Not for a while, I'm afraid."

"Why not? Can't you bring him here? You know where he is."

Jade sighed. "Because I need him to do something for me, Molly, and he can't do it here. It's something very, very important, that only he can do." She leaned forward and laid a cool hand over Molly's hand. "I didn't want to have to do it this way, but I have no choice. Please, I need you to understand, Molly."

It was hard to resist the earnestness in her voice and eyes. This was a very different Snow Queen than the calm, collected being that oversaw the Ball every year. Molly bit her lip. "Why Drew?"

"Because he's a good man," Jade said softly. "And he loves you. That's what I need, a good man to...to prove that there are still good men left." She shook her head. "I can't say any more, but I promise you, I will explain everything afterwards. The big thing is that Drew agreed, on the condition that you agree as well." She leaned back and reached down to the bag she'd been carrying under her cloak. "He wanted me to tell you that he's thinking of you, and he knows you will understand, and that he loves you."

Molly accepted the silver-beaded ball numbly. It was cold, as if it had been formed of the snow falling from the sky outside, and instead of Drew's normal red envelope, there was a scrap of ribbon attached on which he had written, "Don't Despair" in his lovely calligraphy. She turned it over to see that he written "I'll be back as soon as I can" in normal script on the reverse.

"You can't tell me what he's doing."

"No," Jade said. "I'm sorry. But I can promise you that it's important."

"And dangerous?"

"Possibly," Jade said reluctantly. "I'm going to keep him as safe as I can, Molly. I promise you that."

"Can you bring him a message from me?" Molly said finally, after the silence had stretched for a few minutes, broken only by the crackling of the fire in the fireplace.

"Of course."

"Tell him he owes me a Christmas tree." It was stupid, but it was the only thing she could think of that wouldn't have her bawling. Molly raised her chin. "And that he better be back by Christmas Eve."

Jade smiled. "Done."

Chapter 5
December 5

"So wait a minute," Sue Elder said, looking over at Molly. All three of the Terrible Trio, her best friends in the Cove, had descended on the tea shop that afternoon, anxious to hear the story for themselves. The town was rife with rumors as to what had happened the day before, as Molly had known it would be. The Snow Queen (Jade, she reminded herself, and wasn't that weird to know her by her first name) dragging someone off for a private conversation was not a normal thing. Add to that the fact that Drew was still missing, and the Gate where he had been was still inaccessible, and there were speculations running through the town faster than the snow melts in the spring rains. "She had one of the ornaments? How?"

"I assume she got it from Drew," Molly said, scooping up a handful of cinnamon candies from the bowl next to her. She began to press them into the frosting of the snowman cookies on the tray in front of her.

She didn't miss the looks they exchanged over her head, however, and wondered who was supposed to have delivered the ornament instead. And how surprised that person had been to get a visit from the Snow Queen.

"Did you ask her?" Noemi Miller said.

"No," Molly said. "She had already told me she couldn't tell me why she needed him, only that she did need him."

"Do you know what your problem is, Molly?" Lai asked impatiently, sneaking a few M&Ms from another one of the bowls. "You are too damn nice."

"You've told me that before." Molly put another button on a snowman. "Why does it continue to surprise you?"

"Surprise me? No. Irritate me, yes," Lai said. "Why didn't you push her on it?"

"Because she said she couldn't tell me," Molly said.

"And you believed her?" Lai sounded incredulous.

"Why wouldn't I?" Molly finally looked up at her friends. "What good would it do for her to lie to me? What would be the point?" Then she grinned. "Unless, of course, you think she's keeping him as a boy toy or something."

"She could! He's cute!" Lai said.

"He's at least three hundred years younger than she is, too," Noemi said, trying hard not to chuckle. "Talk about an age difference. Then again, maybe she likes them young."

Lai glared at the three of them, all trying to stifle giggles, then finally cracked a smile. "Okay, well, maybe not," she said grudgingly. "But still! What could she want him to do?"

"I don't know," Molly said, going back to her snowmen. "Something she can't do. Schrodinger and I tried to figure it out all last night. He said she's got her fingers in more of the Realms than he could even imagine, and given his imagination, that's a lot. So who knows." She shrugged. "What else can I do, but wait for him to come back?"

And that stung. Molly hated waiting.

"Maybe we could figure out what she needs him for," Sue said.

"To what point?" Molly said, pressing the last button into place. She hadn't mentioned the possible danger Drew was in. That was something that didn't need to get around the Cove.

"She said she needed him to do something important for her and that he'd be back as soon as he was done."

She dropped the remaining cinnamon candies back into the bowl and picked up one of her icing bags. Each snowman needed a green and red scarf next.

"Well, maybe we could help him, so he can come back sooner!" Lai insisted.

Molly painted another green stripe. "And maybe we could mess everything up by blundering in."

Schrodinger had been sitting in the corner of the room, watching and listening. Now he said, *You know, we might be able to help without actually interfering. We just need some more information first.*

All four of them turned to him.

"How?" Noemi said finally, since no one else seemed able to speak.

I can do some nosing around, he said. *There are ways to move around the Realms that don't include the Roads or Gates, and we CrossCats are some of the best at moving unseen when we want to do so. Besides, I know some people.*

Molly was torn. On the one hand, not knowing what Drew was dealing with was maddening. But Jade had been so worried when she'd talked about it. What if Schrodinger got caught? Would it be worth it?

I'm not that easy to catch, Schrodinger said, coming over and rubbing his head against her leg.

"I can't stop you from going," she said, putting down the icing bag and kneeling to hug him. "You're your own person. But remember, you promised Santa you'd be good. And part of being good is being safe." She buried her face in his fur. "I don't know what I'd do if you got hurt looking into this for me."

I'll be extra careful, he promised. *I miss him too.*

✳✳✳

Drew scowled at the falling snow outside and let the curtain drop back down, covering the window. The door to his room wasn't locked anymore; even the front door was unlocked now, but as he had given his word, it didn't really matter.

Three weeks. At the very least, this was going to be his home for three weeks, while he tried to convince a possibly unhinged spirit not to start rampaging through the Cove. And he had to do it without Molly's help. Molly, who was so much better at this than he was.

He wondered again why Jade hadn't approached Molly to help. *Then again, would you want to have her kidnapped and held here? The Cove would implode.* The very thought chilled him. *No, better me than her.*

If I can just figure out how, that is.

Jade had told him that Old Man Winter would come to him, to test him, whatever that meant. Until then, he was twiddling his thumbs in the most luxurious prison he'd ever seen.

He wandered downstairs and into the library, which he'd discovered earlier. There was even a computer attached to the Internet, but he hadn't gotten on, because the temptation to email Molly was too great. And Jade had been adamant that Molly not be involved.

"I will deliver messages to her if you need," the Snow Queen had said, when he'd given her the small ball. "You can continue to communicate with those who are giving the ornaments to her - this is important, and I don't want to take that away from her too. But you cannot communicate with her directly. That could put her in terrible danger."

And that was something he would avoid at all costs.

Drew sat down in front of the computer and tapped out a quick email to Aunt Margie, just verifying that she had received the package he'd sent to her attention. It took all of three seconds for him to receive a reply.

Where are you? He could almost hear the worry in Aunt Margie's voice as he read the email. *When are you coming home? I've got the package, but she needs you here. Please respond.*

Not soon enough, he typed back. *But I'll be in touch. I'm safe. Just don't tell Molly you can contact me, please. It's for her own good.*

After a minute, another email popped up. *You have a lot of explaining to do when you get back, young man.*

Drew chuckled ruefully at the truth in that one sentence, and then went over to the couch. Now, there was nothing to do but wait for Old Man Winter.

I just wish I could be with Molly while I did it, he thought. *We had so many things planned...and now, she'll have to do them alone or with Schrodinger.*

Then an idea tickled at the back of his head. Drew sat up, wondering if he dared. *It would keep her mind off me. And I wouldn't have to worry about her coming after me if she's busy.*

Of course, this could blow up in my face.

But what have I got to lose?

✳✱✳

He was waiting for her next to the scrying pool in the courtyard, screened from the cottage by the falling snow. "You're late," he grunted.

"You're lucky I came at all," Jade said sharply. "I'm not accustomed to being summoned like a child."

"If you act like a child, I'll treat you like a child," Old Man Winter said. "Besides, this is important." He stabbed a finger at the image in the pool. "Condone this, if you can."

Jade leaned in and then shuddered. The scene he'd conjured was one of horror, although it had clearly once been a tranquil village. Now, crimson blood replaced green grass, and burnt-out husks of buildings belched smoke into the skies. As she watched, a human male dragged a screaming child from the shell of a home by an arm.

"Where is this?" she whispered, the blood draining from her face.

"Ashla," he said, and spit on the ground. "Or what used to be Ashla. Now, there's nothing left."

She watched the child being led away to a cart, where others were held in a cage. Slavers. "You could help them," she said.

"Why? They deserve everything they get."

"They're children. They've just seen their parents murdered!" Jade looked up at him. "How can you just stand there and watch this?"

"What would you have me do, Jade? Take them in and raise them myself, so they can do the same thing in ten years? No, thank you."

"You can't just let them go!" she said.

Old Man Winter glanced at the image in the scrying pool. "Fine."

It happened too fast for her to stop. From out of nowhere, large silver wolves sprang out, ripping and mauling everything in their path. The pool did not convey sound, but her imagination supplied the screams.

"And now they don't suffer," he said, and stomped away.

*** ✱ ***

Molly finally threw the Trio out, promising to tell them as soon as Schrodinger came back with any information. "I have work to do!" she told them. "Unless you are going to help me decorate cookies for the school bake sale tomorrow, you need to get out. I need to concentrate!"

They'd gone, promising to come back later and help her pack the cookies into boxes for the next day. Molly had breathed a sigh of relief once the quiet had descended. She turned up the radio, since WCOV (Carter's Cove's own radio station) was broadcasting their recording of the St. Michael's Christmas concert from last year. Starsha, the lovely singer studying in the Cove, had had a starring role--her exquisite voice flowed from the speakers, filling the kitchen with music.

Molly picked up her icing bag again and went back to her decorating, making scarves on the sugar cookies she'd glazed white earlier. Then, while the red and green scarves hardened, she picked up another icing bag, this one filled with black icing. She filled in the top hats and added button eyes and smiles, and pipes to each cookie. Then she went back to the red and green icing, making a festive holly sprig on each hat. Finally, she picked up the orange icing bag for the last touch: the carrot nose. Then on to the next tray, starting once again with cinnamon buttons.

She had nearly eight dozen cookies to decorate and slide into clear cellophane bags placed on trays around the room, and the steady, delicate work distracted her from worrying about Drew and Schrodinger. It was like meditation--clearing out her mind of garbage, leaving only stillness and concentration. When she finally stood up and put the icing bag down after the last cookie, Molly was surprised to find it was nearly four in the afternoon.

"Is it safe?" Aunt Margie asked, poking her head around the kitchen door and grinning at her niece.

"Yes," Molly said, placing all the icing bags into an empty bowl. She dropped the bowl into the sink and filled it with hot water, then turned to face her aunt. "Tea?"

"Please."

As Molly went into the pantry to get another mug, Aunt Margie looked around at the cookies. "These look great!" she called out. "The kids will love them!"

Molly heard a tray move and grinned. *Gotcha, you sneak.* "I hope so," she called back. "Any specific tea request?"

"Surprise me," Aunt Margie answered, her voice a little muffled. "As long as it has caffeine."

Molly suppressed the urge to get something horribly

decaffeinated and plucked a box of her aunt's favorite spiced chai from the shelf. She put a tea bag in the large stoneware mug she'd chosen, then called out, "Can I come out yet, or have you not finished that cookie?"

"You have sharper ears than Schrodinger!" Aunt Margie complained, laughing a bit. "Yes, you can come out."

There was a small brown package waiting for her on the island next to the last tray she'd finished decorating, which was missing a cookie. Molly ignored the box for a moment, picking up her own empty cup on the way to the stove. She put both mugs down, took a tea bag from the ceramic tea house cookie jar that Drew and Schrodinger had gotten her for her birthday, dropped the tea into her mug, and poured boiling water over both tea bags. Then she refilled the kettle, set it back on the flame, and brought both mugs back to the island.

"That smells wonderful." Aunt Margie accepted the mug with a sigh of relief.

"It would go well with another cookie," Molly said, sliding one on to a plate and grinning.

"I won't say no," Aunt Margie agreed.

After moving the rest of the tray out of temptation's reach, Molly sat down across from her aunt. "Where did this come from?" she asked, indicating the box.

"It came in the afternoon mail," Aunt Margie said. "Be careful. It's marked fragile."

Molly picked it up and raised one eyebrow. It was heavier than she'd thought it would be, considering the size. The return address was the Gate Station, with the words "Gate Delivery" on it. Which meant it had come from somewhere else.

Inside was a gaily wrapped box, the silver and gold paisley paper brilliant in the kitchen light. Molly unwrapped it carefully and opened the plain sturdy white box she found within. She pulled out a wad of green tissue paper, then gasped.

Nestled in more tissue paper was a china teacup with a small ornament inside it. Molly lifted the cup out, marveling at the thinness of the china. Hand-painted holly leaves and gold edging sparkled; she wondered how old it was, and where Drew had found it. There was a matching saucer, of course. Then she finally found the familiar red envelope.

Aunt Margie took the ornament from the cup. "These are amazing," she said. It was red and gold, and like the others, was tiny. Just the right size for the little tree Drew had left on Molly's dining room table.

"I know," Molly said, opening the card. "I don't know where he found them."

The card said, "No matter where I go, I see you everywhere. I saw this and knew it had to be yours. I'll see you drinking out of it soon enough. Love, Drew."

Molly closed the card and put it back in the box. Then she moved the precious cup and saucer to a shelf where she could see it, but it wouldn't be hit accidentally.

"He'll be back, child," Aunt Margie said softly. "He'll be back."

"I know," Molly said, returning to her seat, still looking at the tea cup on its shelf. "I know."

✳✱✳

Old Man Winter paced along a Road, two large wolves at his side. They were snapping and snarling at the air, reacting to the anger churning through his mind. He still had to figure out how to test the boy fairly.

Then again, their whole species regularly lies and cheats. Why should I play fair?

The voice in his head started to whisper a plan, one destined to make sure the boy would fail spectacularly. And then he could tell Jade to go to hell, and take her beloved Cove with her.

But then another voice, a voice he hadn't heard in a very long time, spoke up. *If you cheat, you are no better than they are,* it said, quiet and weak, but still audible. He'd thought that voice dead a long time ago. *Which proves her point.*

We ARE better than them, the first voice snapped. *We have nothing to prove.*

His head ached. Too many voices. There were too many voices these days.

Hopefully that would be resolved when he destroyed the Cove.

And then he heard another voice, one that wasn't from within his head, raised in pain and fear, and he started to run.

Chapter 6
December 6

*B*ang!

The slamming of the front door jolted Drew from sleep. He lay there a moment longer, dazed, wondering what he'd heard. Then heavy footsteps clomped across the front hall and up the stairs. Whoever it was, it wasn't the dainty Snow Queen.

He slipped from the bed and padded in his bare feet across the room to the door. It was still early; the sun was barely above the horizon, and the long rays only reached halfway across the bedroom, so the area by the door was still in shadow. Drew flattened himself against the wall next to the door as the footsteps came closer to his room. It was obvious whoever it was wasn't concerned about being heard.

The door opened, and the giant who had kidnapped him stepped into the room, still dressed in furs. Drew frowned.

This is Old Man Winter?

"Good, you're up," Old Man Winter said, turning around and looking at him. "Get dressed. We're going for a walk."

"Is this the test you're going to give me?" Drew asked. "To prove to you why you shouldn't destroy Carter's Cove."

Old Man Winter didn't say anything. He just crossed his arms and waited.

"Fine. Be that way." Drew went over to the dresser. He looked over his shoulder. "You going to stay and watch me dress?"

"Modest, boy?" Old Man Winter snorted, but turned to leave. "I'll meet you in the front hall. Dress warmly."

"Where are we going?" Drew asked, opening a drawer at random.

"Out," Old Man Winter said, and left.

"Well, that's informative," Drew grumbled, and went looking for his wool socks.

When he came down the stairs, Old Man Winter handed him a pack. "Here, take this. And follow me."

After more than an hour of walking, Drew still had no idea where they were going. He was carrying a heavy pack, weighted down with God knew what, and following Old Man Winter on something that might have been a path in a former life. The spirit had his own pack, as big as Drew's, but it didn't seem to slow him down at all.

The only thing Drew was sure of was that at least part of the journey had been on a Road, although they hadn't gone through a Gate. Old Man Winter didn't need them, apparently; he'd just grabbed Drew's arm and taken an extra step, and that was that.

They'd stepped off the Road the same way, into another snowy wilderness that may or may not have been the Snow Queen's domain. The sun was up and sparkling on snow that looked like it had never had human footprints on it.

He was just about to ask Old Man Winter a question when the spirit stopped and held up his hand. "Wait, and don't move."

Drew tensed and looked around. "Why?"

"Because I don't want you to scare her," Old Man Winter snapped. "Stay here while I go in. Come when I call you. And don't get any ideas about taking off. We're not alone."

As if to underscore that statement, a wolf howled, far closer than Drew had ever heard them. The sound shivered through him like an icy wind.

Old Man Winter gave him one last piercing look, then continued up the game trail. As he waited, Drew realized that other than the sounds of the wolves and branches being moved aside, he couldn't hear anything else. It was the quietest woods he'd ever been in.

"All right," he heard, after about fifteen minutes. "You can come back, but do it slowly. She's in a lot of pain and not inclined to be charitable now."

Drew pushed his way up through the underbrush along the trail. Fir tree branches scratched against his face and arms, filling the air with their heady fragrance. Finally, he broke into a small clearing and saw who "she" was.

Old Man Winter was seated in the snow. Curled half in the old man's lap was the smallest dragon Drew had ever seen. Of course, it was the only dragon he'd ever seen, but still. He'd thought they'd be...bigger.

This dragon was about the size of a large wolf, or a small adult deer; she was sprawled in the snow, her front legs and jewel-toned head resting in the old man's lap. Her wings were furled against her sinuous body, and she glimmered in the sunlight. All in all, she was breathtaking.

"Carefully," Old Man Winter warned as Drew stepped into the clearing. "Don't startle her."

The dragon's head had shot up as the young tech came into the small glade; her sapphire eyes fastened on him, freezing him in place. The faintest wisp of blue-grey smoke rose from one of her nostrils.

Drew saw why she was in pain immediately. Somehow she'd been caught in an old bear trap: the rusted iron teeth of the medieval device had sunk right through her magical scales, biting deeply into her flesh. Old Man Winter was supporting her, taking pressure off the affected leg, but keeping well away from the iron. *Which is why he needs me,* Drew realized. *I'm the only one who can take the touch of the iron.*

But what the hell was this thing doing out here?

Moving slowly, the way he had back on his grandparents' farm around the horses they'd bred, Drew knelt down next to the dragon, trying not to flinch back from the feel of her gaze boring into his back. He eased the pack down, shed his gloves, and reached out to lay a hand on the trap.

"Easy, girl," he said quietly as he felt her flinch. "I'm not going to hurt you." He continued to talk in the same calm, soothing voice he'd used on his grandfather's prized Percherons as he ran his fingertips around the edges of the wound, wincing inwardly at the damage. The teeth had barely missed severing her leg, and he could already see the beginning signs of iron poisoning. They would have to work fast.

"Can you get it off, boy?" Old Man Winter asked, using the same calm, quiet voice Drew had. He was stroking the dragon's head. Other than a slight trembling of her body, she hadn't moved, and Drew saw as he turned slightly that she was still watching him intently.

"Depends on what tools we brought." Drew sat back on his heels. "And if she lets me put any pressure on the trap."

Do what you need to, young one. The voice in his head was softer, lighter than Schrodinger's, but it rang with a resonance the CrossCat's mental tone lacked. *I will endure.*

Drew dared to lay a hand on her flank, well away from the wounds. "I'll be as careful as I can be," he promised. Then he turned his attention to the packs. Old Man Winter had packed well--there was a large set of bolt cutters, as well as plenty of bandages and tubes of ointment. He pulled out the cutters first, and positioned them on the edge of one of the trap's jaws, targeting the hinges.

One quick snap, and the iron sang as the edges of the metal

parted. The next cut would be the tricky one. He stood up and, moving slowly, straddled her leg so he could get the other hinge. Another snap, and Drew tossed the bolt cutters aside.

Before he started to pull the trap off, Drew knelt down beside her again. He couldn't just lift it off--whoever had built the wretched thing had serrated the teeth, which meant her scales and flesh were tangled within the metal. If he lifted it recklessly, he could still sever her leg.

"This is going to be the painful part," he warned her. "I'm going to go slowly, but it's going to hurt. I promise I'll be as gentle as I can."

"The silver tube has a numbing agent in it," Old Man Winter told him. "Smear that on before you start."

Drew did so, feeling the dragon's scales shiver under his touch. Then he settled down in the snow and began the delicate, tedious task of removing the trap from her flesh.

It felt like hours later when he untangled the last tooth from her leg, and lifted the top of the iron trap away. He stowed it in his pack, then looked at his companions.

"In order to get the other part off, we're going to have to move you," he said to the dragon. "The other part of the trap is going to be even more embedded. Are you okay with moving?"

Yes, the dragon said, after a moment's consideration. *But I will need help.*

Between the two of them, Old Man Winter and Drew managed to turn her over with a minimum of jostling to her injured leg. In his mind, Drew kept seeing Schrodinger or Jack or one of the other animals from the Cove caught in the cruel metal, and rage grew in his chest. *What kind of monster sets traps like this?*

Old Man Winter spat on the ground next to him, away from the dragon. "Same kind that brings unrest. Those that care only about themselves, about making money, and damn who it hurts. You know, most of your species."

They are not the majority of humans, as you well know, Old Man, the dragon said, laying her head back in his lap. *Most humans will help, not hurt.*

"Not enough of them," the old man said darkly.

That is not true, and you know it.

"Bah."

Drew bent his head over her leg, his mind working fast as his fingers methodically unwound the iron from her flesh. The back and forth seemed to indicate a conversation that had been going on for a while. Was that why she'd been targeted for the trap? Or had she just been unlucky?

"Where are we?" he asked. "What Realm, I mean?"

"Why?" Old Man Winter looked sharply at him. "Thinking of making a run for it?"

"Hardly," Drew said. "I made a bargain. But we need to report this trap being set."

"What good will reporting it do?"

"The people who set it need to be punished," Drew said.

Old Man Winter chuckled, and the sound chilled Drew's blood. "Oh, they will be."

Drew tried not to shiver at the mayhem implicit in that statement. He straightened up and looked at the dragon. "How long have you been here?"

Overnight, she admitted. *I was surprised by the trap. It was hidden well, and the shock of the wound knocked me out for several hours. I was lucky that I recovered enough to send a message to Old Man Winter.* She nosed Drew's shoulder. *And luckier still that you were able to come and help.*

"It's my pleasure," he told her. "I'm just sorry it was necessary."

"It won't be again," Old Man Winter said, and Drew heard the wolves howl again. "Not for these particular humans, anyways."

Just remember, Old Man, that not every human in that village sets traps, the dragon said reprovingly.

"But how did they know to set it here?" Drew said.

My home is over the hills to the north, she said. *I often walk through here - it's pleasant, especially in the evenings.*

"Which means they set it for you specifically." That made Drew sick. "Why?"

Dragon's blood is a powerful magical tool, and the village is poor. They've fallen on hard times lately. I don't doubt that someone offered them quite a lot of money for whatever they could get. She sighed. *I just wish they had asked me for help. I would have gladly given them some of my scales to sell.*

"Humans don't ask. They take. Arrogant bastards." Old Man Winter spat again.

Drew bent his head back over his work, processing that information. He'd known about the black market, of course, but he'd never been this directly impacted by it. And had the Snow Queen arranged this? Could she be that cold?

This is not Jade's doing, the dragon said quietly, and he was certain Old Man Winter could not hear them. *She will be horrified, and more so at his response. This was not the test she had in mind.* There was a great sadness in her voice. *I can only hope that she can rein him in before he goes in search of the hunters. But I don't know that she will.*

✳✱✳

"So, what did you find out?" Molly asked, cradling her tea mug in her hand. She and Schrodinger were hanging out in the living room after eating breakfast. The CrossCat was curled up on one of his cat beds, taking a leisurely bath. Molly was still in her pajamas, sitting in her wing chair with one leg slung over the arm. It was quiet in the apartment; a waiting stillness that was somehow languid and enervating at the same time hung in the air.

Schrodinger didn't answer at first, concentrating on his right hind leg. Molly recognized the fact that he was collecting his thoughts and wondered just where he had gone the day before. He hadn't come back until after she'd gotten home from the bookstore, and he'd been tired; he'd nearly fallen asleep over his dinner, and Molly had ended up carrying him into bed. So she waited now, knowing he would tell her in his own time.

I went to see the Librarian, he said finally, finishing his bath. He jumped out of his bed and trotted over to her, waiting until she rearranged herself to jump into her lap.

"Who's the Librarian?" she asked, pulling a blanket up from the floor so they could cuddle together.

She was my teacher, Schrodinger said, snuggling down. *The wisest of all the CrossCats in the Realms. Also, my great-great-grandmother.*

"What did she say?" Molly loved to hear Schrodinger talk about his family. "And why did you go to see her?"

Because there is very little that goes on in the Realms that she doesn't know about. She listens, and people tell her things. All sorts of things. And she said there are dark things moving lately. Schrodinger paused. *She said the Snow Queen has been very busy lately, trying to settle something.*

"Settle something?"

Yes. The Librarian said there has been dissent in the Realms. Old angers boiling over. Old hatreds coming to light.

Molly thought about whatever had been destroying Gates over the past year, and how Drew had said there seemed to be more territorial disputes rising. "But what does that have to do with Drew?" she asked. "Do you think she needs him to be a diplomat, maybe?"

I don't know. Schrodinger crossed his front paws and put his chin down on them. *But the Librarian also said that Old Man Winter has been seen again.*

"Who?"

Old Man Winter, Schrodinger repeated. *I've heard a lot of stories about him, but no one seems to know exactly who he is. Some say he's the Snow Queen's father, some others say they are brother and sister. He's been around as long as anyone can remember, and legend says that he brings the winter winds and snows to the Realms. He hasn't been seen for a long time, though. Usually, we just hear his winds. Or, if it's been a harsh winter, his wolves.*

"His wolves?" Molly shivered. "Those sound dangerous."

They are, which is why they are so feared, Schrodinger agreed. *They bring the wildest winter storms, so the legends say, and I don't know of anyone who has encountered them and lived to tell about it. But the Librarian said Old Man Winter and his wolves were spotted out on the Roads two days ago, hunting. She said that the last time he went hunting with his wolves, an entire village vanished.*

"That's when Drew went missing," Molly said. "Do you think Jade wants him to deal with Old Man Winter?"

It could be.

Molly stroked Schrodinger's head as she thought. "Jade said he was doing something very important. And the Gate that Drew was working on still isn't responding."

That I can clear up, Schrodinger said. *I went and checked on it after I left the Librarian. The Road was moved, and not by accident. It was ripped from the Gate.*

"That takes a lot of power, doesn't it? Power that Old Man Winter would have."

Yes. And the way station was saturated with an icy presence. Not the Snow Queen's presence.

Molly sighed. "I wish I knew what was going on. We've got bits and pieces, but not the whole."

Old Man Winter coming back is worrying the Librarian, Schrodinger said. *She said he has changed, that he hunts more now than he had in the past.*

"Did she say what he was hunting?"

No, he said. *But that's even worse. What if he's hunting Drew?*

Molly sighed. "I can't think anymore right now," she said, nudging him off her lap. "I need a shower before Sue gets here."

Several hours later, Molly stood in front of the Daughter of Stars Middle School. The glass doors were decorated with hundreds of paper snowflakes and snowmen, all created by the children who were even now squirming in their seats, sneaking looks at the clock and counting down the minutes until they were released. She knew exactly where most of them would run at the bell: right into the gymnasium, where dozens of tables were set up, covered with an array of amazing goodies. This was the first year the school had decided to try a Christmas Fair, and to judge by the cars in the parking lot, it was going to be a success.

She looked around inside Sue's car, making sure she wasn't leaving anything behind, and then heaved her last box of decorated cookies out of the trunk. Schrodinger was inside, guarding the tables with Sue. It was supposed to have been Drew helping her, but, well...

We work with what we have, Molly thought grimly, pushing her way through the double doors. *We can handle this. Luckily, Sue was able to get the time to come and help on short notice.*

She'd done more than just show up--Sue had brought tablecloths and placards with prices on them, all done up in brilliant Christmas colors. While Molly was getting the last of the cookies from the car, Sue and Schrodinger had claimed their three tables and spread out the cranberry red and evergreen plaid tablecloths. One of the totes held silver serving trays; as Molly set down her box, Sue was already laying them out on the tables.

"I figured I could do this," she said, as Molly looked over the arrangements. "I haven't touched the actual cookies yet, in case you wanted to change it."

"That's fine." Molly stepped out into the aisle and looked at the tables from the front with a critical eye. "It looks great so far!"

Sue had put the large apothecary jars Molly had collected

along the back of the tables, except for the corner where she'd put the cash box and a sign that said "CrossWinds Tea Shop." The silver trays went across the front, ready for cookies.

"Here, please put the candy canes in the jars," Molly said, handing her the box. Then Molly started to lay out the snowflakes and snowmen cookies. She and Schrodinger had put their heads together to figure out exactly what kind of cookies they should bring, and had decided on the peppermint candy canes, sugar cookie snowmen, and gingerbread snowflakes. In addition, there was a gingerbread cottage that was to promote the gingerbread houses Molly offered for the holidays.

"Oh, that reminds me, I made these for you too," Sue said, passing a small stack of papers to Molly, who took them with a puzzled look on her face.

"What--OH! Thank you!"

They were order forms, done in the same colors as the price cards, for Molly's Christmas goodies. Every year, she took orders for cookies, cakes, scones, and other baked goods, and every year, she'd sworn she was going to make order forms for them. She never had. "What would I do without you?" she said now, giving Sue a quick hug. "They're perfect!"

Sue beamed. "And I have the template saved, so we can make more next year." She also produced a couple of clipboards with candy cane pens attached. "I borrowed these from the museum too. I thought we could use them."

"I should hire you to be my business manager," Molly said, laughing.

"I work cheap," Sue replied. "I'll settle for payment in cookies."

"I can do that!"

And then, from above, a harsh familiar buzzer sounded, and Molly and Sue went behind the tables.

It was a mob scene, and after taking a look, Schrodinger decided the best place for him was behind the tables so he didn't get stepped on. Families wound through the passages created by the tables, oohing and aahing over the variety of goods available. Molly's cookies went quickly, as she knew they would, and Sue's forms were just as quickly filled out.

"We're going to busy in the next few weeks," Molly said to Schrodinger, looking at the pile of forms in Sue's hands as the crowds began to thin. "How many of those did you print?"

"Only 50, and of those, only 20 are gingerbread houses," Sue said. "I didn't want to overwhelm you. Aunt Margie would murder me."

"Thank goodness," Molly said.

"Molly?"

They all turned at the sound of the voice. There was a little girl (well, not as little has she had been, Molly realized) standing in front of the table, her pale blue eyes looking past them, her delicate face alight with excitement.

Sarah! Schrodinger leaped out from the tables and snuggled up carefully to the girl, who leaned down unerringly and hugged him. *I was hoping you'd come!*

"Of course I'd come," she told him, her fingers traveling over his fuzzy face in greeting. "I have something to do."

"You do?" Molly asked.

Sarah nodded. "It will only take a minute," she said. "I have to do it quickly, before Dad comes over."

Considering her father was Police Sargent Jamie Carter, Molly grinned. "I have an idea what it is then," she said, and Sarah giggled. "How many this year?"

"Mom said we could get two this year, since Uncle Joshua and Aunt Carolyn are coming for Christmas, and I'd like to make one a Christmas tree, if I could," Sarah said.

"We can do a gingerbread Christmas tree," Molly said, writing down the order. "Did you want the other one to be a regular gingerbread house?"

"Could you do the Gate station?" Sarah asked wistfully. "Mom says it's beautiful."

"Of course!" It would take a bit more gingerbread than the normal house, but for Sarah, Molly would do it. The little blind girl was one of her favorites too. "For the week before Christmas?"

"Yes, please." Sarah held out not only a check, but a small box. "And could you please use this as a template for the ornaments on the tree?"

Taking the box, Molly nodded. "Okay." Then she saw the red envelope as she lifted the lid. "Oh, Sarah, you too?"

Sarah grinned. "Is it pretty? Drew said they were all pretty."

Molly lifted out the envelope, and then pulled out the ornament. This one was gold with pearl beads interspersed in the webbing. "It's beautiful," she said, placing the little ornament in the girl's hand. "All gold and bits of pearl. It glows like a snowflake at night."

"It sounds lovely," Sarah told her, running her fingers over the webbing. Then she handed the ornament back. "I can't wait to see the tree."

"I'll make it shine," Molly said.

Sarah turned to leave, but then turned back, her sightless eyes wise. "He'll be back, Molly. He said to tell you he loves you, and that he knows you'd help if you could."

He knows you'd help if you could. Molly stiffened. That wasn't what she'd expected to hear.

But it was true. Even in the rush of the Christmas Fair, she'd been turning over ways in her mind to try and help him. To get him home sooner.

"You're right," she said. "I would."

Sarah smiled and then ran off.

What are you thinking? Schrodinger asked her.

"I don't know yet," Molly said, looking at the little ornament in her hand. "I don't know."

Chapter 7
December 7

"**A**m I late?"

Lai rushed into the kitchen, her bag banging on her hip. "I'm so sorry!" she continued breathlessly. "I had a conference call run long!"

"You're fine," Molly said, setting a tea cup and saucer in front of her. "We haven't started yet."

"Oh good." Lai sank down on the stool and looked at the others. Noemi, Sue, and Schrodinger were perched on their own stools, and Molly was standing in her normal spot between the island and the ovens. She put a stainless steel tea ball in the cup in front of Lai, then poured boiling water over it. Fragrant steam rose up from the cup, joining with the other scents of tea and chai and cider. "I was worried you'd start without me."

"No, we wouldn't." Molly looked around at them and then did something she'd never done before: she went and locked the kitchen door. For the next twenty minutes, nothing would go in or out.

"All right," she said, clicking the lock and turning back to her friends. "Nothing we say here goes outside."

The Trio looked at her a bit apprehensively. Schrodinger, who already knew what she was going to say, lapped up a bit of tea.

"What I'm going to say needs to not go further than this room," she warned them. "I'm about to possibly cross one of the biggest influences in the Realms, and if you don't want to go with me, I won't blame you. Just let me know now, and I'll let you out."

For a couple of minutes, the room was quiet except for the ticking of the clock and the strains of Christmas carols from the radio she kept on a shelf near the door. Then Sue broke the silence.

"No," she said firmly. "We're in this together." Noemi and Lai nodded

You know I'm not going anywhere, Schrodinger said. *So let's get started.*

"You guys are the best," Molly said, and meant it. She went back to the island and cupped her hands around her tea mug. "Okay, here's the deal."

Between the two of them, she and Schrodinger filled the Trio in on what they'd found out.

"So you think Old Man Winter kidnapped Drew to what...force him to help him destroy the Cove's Gate?" Noemi asked, her eyes wide.

"No," Molly said. "I think the Snow Queen set Drew up to be kidnapped, to give him a chance to change Old Man Winter's mind from whatever he has planned."

"Wow." Sue sat back, clearly stunned. "That's kind of cold."

She's more than just a figurehead who throws a good party, Schrodinger said. *She rules her own Realm and she's influential in thousands more. If she needs to sacrifice one person to save an entire Realm, or group of Realms, she will. But I don't think that's what she's doing.*

"So what do you think she's doing?" Lai asked him. "Do you really think she thinks Drew can change Old Man Winter's mind?"

Maybe. I think it more likely that she thinks Molly can.

"Molly?" Sue said, shocked. "How?"

"What are you planning?" Lai asked at the same time.

Molly raised her chin. "I'm going to challenge Old Man Winter."

"What??"

All three of them stared at her in horrified admiration, and she giggled a bit in spite of herself. "Not like that, guys! You should know me better than that! I'm not a fighter."

"So what are you going to do?" Noemi said. "Assuming you can find him."

I can find anyone, Schrodinger said.

"And once he does, I'm going to convince Old Man Winter to let Drew go," Molly said.

"Well, at least we know your self-confidence is intact," Lai said after a minute. "Where do we fit into this?"

"I need to know more about Old Man Winter, for one," Molly said. She looked at Sue. "Do you have anything at the museum that might help?"

Sue frowned. "I don't know," she admitted. "There are some archives that I've never been in that might hold some information. I have the keys to them, but the Director seems to prefer that they stay forgotten."

"I can help you go through them, if you like," Noemi offered. "I'm on break for the next two weeks."

"Sounds good," Sue said. She looked at Molly. "We can start this afternoon, if you want."

"Do so, please," Molly said. "Schrodinger's going to start looking for Old Man Winter."

The CrossCat's tail swished. *And I'll find him, too. No one can hide from me for long. Even Old Man Winter.*

Molly stroked his head fondly. "Just remember, you need to be careful and make sure his wolves don't catch you."

They won't. I'm too fast.

"And what is Schrodinger going to do once he finds Old Man Winter?" Lai asked.

Molly smiled. "He's going to invite him to tea, of course."

✳✱✳

"She's going to do WHAT?"

Drew stared at the computer screen, aghast. He'd been checking his email, making sure Luke had the next ornament ready to go, when the message from Father Christopher asking him to an instant messenger session had popped up. Since the only person he'd been forbidden to communicate directly with was Molly, he'd clicked on the link. Now he was regretting it.

"That's what Margie said," Father Christopher told him. "Since Molly never locks the kitchen door, it piqued her curiosity. Especially considering who was in there with her."

Drew sat back in the chair, stunned. "She's looking for Old Man Winter."

"That's what Margie said," Father Christopher repeated. "And honestly, I'm not surprised. Are you?"

"No," Drew admitted. "And that's what scares me."

"What are we going to do with her, Drew?"

"I don't know, but I'll work on it," Drew said. "Thank you for letting me know. And see if you can distract her."

"I'll do my best."

Once the priest had signed off, Drew stared at the blank screen for a few minutes, wondering what the heck he was going to do now. In all honesty, he was surprised she hadn't already shown up at the door, and the Snow Queen's request be damned. But this...this was far worse than anything he'd thought she'd do.

He pulled up his email program again and tapped out a quick note. "You still coming tomorrow? Things have gotten worse. D."

After a few moments, a reply popped up. "They always do. Docking at mid-morning, will be there soon as I can. P."

With a sigh, Drew got up and wandered out into the hallway, heading for the courtyard behind the house. He and Old Man Winter had carried the dragon out of the clearing to find a sleigh waiting for them, a long dog-sled type vehicle. No dogs, though-- Drew and Old Man Winter had pulled the sled back to the cottage, trying their best not to jar the dragon's injured leg or work too much magic around her. The iron would have to be leeched out of her flesh slowly, Old Man Winter had said, and until then, magic had to be kept to a minimum.

They'd brought her into the stables, where there were huge box stalls full of soft straw. No horses, but plenty of stalls, and the dragon fit perfectly in one.

Drew went out there now, shrugging into a heavy flannel shirt as he did so. The dragon preferred cold temperatures, so the stable was minimally heated.

You are troubled. Her blue eyes were as calm as her mental voice. *Something is worrying you.*

"My girlfriend is trying to rescue me," Drew said, kneeling down to check the bandages on her leg. Old Man Winter had left the medications and salves in the next stall after giving the young man instructions on what needed to be done to draw out the iron and keep the wounds from getting infected. Now, Drew peeled off the soft cloth, stained red with rust, and peered at the jagged cuts. "No infection," he said approvingly.

Old Man Winter has always been a good healer, regardless of his other actions, she said, watching him spread salve gently on her leg. *As are you.*

"I'm just a good technician," he said, putting the salve aside and picking up a fresh bandage.

You are a good man, Drew McIntyre, she said, dropping her head on his shoulder briefly. *And you are worried. Tell me why. I am a good listener.*

And she was. As he wrapped the new bandage around her leg, Drew shared everything he knew: what he'd planned for Molly for Christmas, how that had been disrupted when the Snow Queen had asked him for help, and what he'd just found out from Father Christopher that Molly was planning. "So now I don't know what to do," he finished. "How can I keep her safe?"

Sometimes you cannot, the dragon said. *Sometimes you have to let her keep you safe. Did you not think of that?*

Drew stopped, looking at her. He'd always wanted to protect Molly. It was in large part why he'd agreed to help the Snow Queen, once he'd known what was going on. But in this instance, maybe he'd have to let her keep him safe.

"Thank you," he said. "For listening."

I am called Ember, she said, inclining her head. *And I am very happy to have met you, Drew McIntyre, although I wish it could have been under different circumstances. I think you have great things ahead of you.*

Then she winked at him. *If you can survive this December, that is.*

✳✳✳

"Molly? Schrodinger?"

Molly heard Luke come into the kitchen as she collected boxes for the scones she'd made earlier. "I'll be out in a second!" she called, reaching for the last stack. Then she came out of the pantry, grinning. "Looking for something hot on your way home from the Station? Or are you headed somewhere else?"

Luke's cheeks were flushed with cold, and he grinned back at her as he shucked his coat. "I won't say no to something hot, but no caffeine, please," he said, putting a passel of bags on the island. "The wind is wicked out tonight! I hope you guys have a ride home."

She nodded as she put a heavy ceramic mug full of steaming cider in front of him. "Aunt Margie won't let me walk home alone."

"Where's Schrodinger?" Luke asked, one eyebrow raised.

"He's off wandering," Molly said, waving one hand vaguely. "He does that from time to time. It might be Christmas shopping, for all I know."

"How does he pay for Christmas shopping?" Luke asked, then flushed. "I mean, does he have money?"

"He barters. Errands, usually," Molly said. "I gather CrossCats have been doing it for centuries. They're really reliable messengers."

"Well, I hope it's warmer wherever he is," Luke said.

Not likely, Molly thought, but smiled at him. "I'm sure he'll tell me all about it when he gets home." She eyed his bags. "Did some Christmas shopping of your own, huh? Is there a black box from Pho's Jewelers in there somewhere?"

He flushed again. "Maybe."

She leaned in. "Can I see?"

Paper crinkled as he reached into one bag and pulled out a long velvet box with Pho's signature snake emblem twined around it. "Do you think Sue will like it?"

"Oh Luke, I think she'll love it." Molly took the box and gazed in awe at the sapphire bracelet nestled into the velvet. "Seriously."

"Awesome." Luke took the bracelet back and grinned at her. "I have something in here for you too."

"Shocking," Molly teased him. "You don't say."

The ornament this time was blue, just like the sapphires in Sue's bracelet, and it was attached to a narrow wrapped box surmounted by a red envelope. She opened the envelope first.

"I was hoping to watch this with you so we could get ready for next week. We'll just have to do a second showing when I get back," she read.

The package contained a DVD of The Nutcracker ballet, and Molly smiled. "He remembered." When Luke looked puzzled, she explained, "Lily is one of the snowflakes in the ballet at the dance school next week. Drew and I..." She faltered a little bit, then recovered. "We have tickets to take Schrodinger."

"I hope Drew's back by then." Luke drained the rest of his cider and shrugged back into his coat. "We're doing everything we can."

So am I, she thought, as he went out the kitchen door. *So am I.*

Chapter 8
December 8

"Well, well, well, you have fallen into a nice nest, haven't you? I thought you said this was a prison!"

The familiar booming voice echoed through the entire house, and Drew grinned. "It's a gilded cage," he said, coming down the stairs. "I'm a golden bird."

"I have heard you sing," the man at the bottom of the stairs snorted. "Golden is not a word I would use to describe it." He looked up at Drew. "And you look surprisingly well for a prisoner. Despite it being ungodly early."

"It's nearly noon, Pavel," Drew said. "It's not exactly early."

"Says you." Pavel shrugged.

Drew shook his head and clapped his old friend on the shoulder. "Although I am surprised to see you this early, to be honest. I was expecting you around mid-afternoon, given your message."

"I made the crew row," Pavel said, shrugging, and then laughed at the shocked look on Drew's face. "I'm kidding! They'd mutiny. But seriously, my friend," and the amusement fell away from his handsome face, "you called. I came. What are friends for?"

"True," Drew agreed. "Follow me. I was just about to make

lunch."

The kitchen in the cottage (Drew couldn't help but call it that, even though it was the biggest cottage he'd ever seen) was as decked out as any he'd ever been in. *Yet another reason to bring Molly out here at some point. She'd love a chance at a kitchen like this.*

As Pavel settled into one of the chairs at the kitchen table, Drew opened the fridge and pulled out sandwich ingredients. The invisible servants who made sure he didn't starve had left him half a ham, already sliced, and some orange marmalade. Drew added in some sliced tomatoes, a bunch of lettuce leaves, and then dug around in the cheese drawer until he found some sliced provolone. He deposited everything in front of Pavel.

"Bread?" the big man asked.

"Working on it," Drew said, moving towards the bread box on the counter. It was white, as was everything in the kitchen, and had disgorged all sorts of goodies in the few days that he'd been here, although not as good as Molly's. Today, it gave him thick slices of a hearty brown bread, enough for two, even given Pavel's appetite.

"This is a good kitchen," Pavel said, taking two of the slices from the plate Drew set down. "I approve."

"I'm sure the Snow Queen will be happy you do," Drew said, sitting down opposite him and putting two beers on the table. "I'd prefer to be back in the Cove, though."

"Prisons, even gilded ones, are still prisons, even if the Snow Queen is a gentle jailer," Pavel said. "So why is she holding you here?"

"That," Drew said, picking up his beer, "is a long story."

As they ate, Drew told him about Old Man Winter and the task that the Snow Queen had put to him. After he was done, Pavel shook his head. "You are in a lot of trouble, my friend."

Drew shrugged. "Not me, really. I'm more concerned about Molly."

"Oh?" Pavel raised an eloquent black eyebrow. "You are here, with Old Man Winter's wolves skulking in the woods nearby, and the Snow Queen's guards at the foot of the hill. Also, you have a dragon in your stable. I say you are the one in trouble, not your lovely lady."

"Guards at the bottom of the hill?" That was news to Drew. "I wonder why."

"Perhaps because the Snow Queen wants to make sure you are not disturbed?" Pavel said. "Once they saw it was me, they did not hinder me."

"Interesting." Drew filed that bit of information away, wondering if the guards were there for him or for Ember. Old Man Winter had been gone for the last few days, and Drew didn't know where. Ember hadn't said. "And how did you know about the dragon?"

"Please, Drew." Pavel gave him a long-suffering look. "I hear things. It's my job."

Drew gave up at that point. "Fine, don't tell me. Here's what I need you to do: deliver a message to Molly for me, and keep her safe. Can you do that?"

"Why don't you invite her out here to give her your message? I'm sure you can think of something to distract her with here, and then she can't find Old Man Winter."

"I can't, remember? I promised the Snow Queen I wouldn't contact her directly." Drew sighed. "I just can't let her take Old Man Winter on herself. She has no idea what she's dealing with."

"She doesn't lack for spirit," Pavel observed, leaning back and lacing his fingers over his stomach as he frowned. His large black mustache drooped over his cheeks. "I was right. You are in a lot of trouble."

"Will you help me or not?" Drew asked.

"Of course I will help you." Pave shrugged. "Trouble is my middle name." He winked at Drew. "Now, what message am I delivering?"

"First you have to go and get it," Drew said, and began to outline what he needed Pavel to do.

✳✱✳

Old Man Winter stood in the shadows of the stable, watching the pirate saunter down the driveway. He was mildly impressed. He hadn't expected the boy to reach out to someone like Pavel Chekhov.

"This could prove inconvenient," he said, mostly to himself.

You mean interesting, don't you? Ember arched her head up over her body to look at him, her blue eyes amused. He scowled at her and she said, *At least you won't be bored.*

"I'm never bored," he snapped, squatting down to inspect her leg. The salve to leech out the iron was working, although it was a slow process. "The boy is conscientious about this, at least."

His name is Drew, and he's been very kind.

He grunted.

Did you know his girlfriend is looking for you?

"Why?"

She sighed. *Because you took her boyfriend during the Christmas season? Because you're threatening her home? Why else?*

"That wasn't the agreement. The agreement was that the boy--"

Drew.

"Drew, then," Old Man Winter snapped, biting the words off. "Drew is the one who has to convince me."

But he won't, will he? Her mental voice was sad. *You're just biding your time, humoring Jade until she turns her back, aren't you?*

"You have no idea what you're talking about," he said.

Am I wrong? She fixed him with a piercing gaze, all amusement gone. *Tell me, Old Man, how many people did you leave alive in the village below my cave?*

He didn't answer her.

✳✳✳

Molly was singing along with Burl Ives as she rolled out gingerbread dough in the kitchen, and to all appearances, she was fine. Happy, if a little worried about Drew, which was completely normal. No one except the Trio suspected that she was worried about more than Drew. Schrodinger had headed out first thing in the morning again to look for Old Man Winter.

Mal had come down earlier that morning and let her know what Schrodinger had already told her: that the Road had moved too much to be used by that Gate again, and that they were abandoning efforts to reconnect it. "But that doesn't mean we're giving up on Drew," he had hastened to assure her. "We just need to go about it a different way."

"You might as well give up," she'd said calmly. "Drew isn't there anymore."

Mal had gaped at her, his ever-present cigarette (unlit in her kitchen, thankfully) nearly falling out of his mouth. "How did you know that?"

"Schrodinger went and looked." There was no reason to lie to the Gate manager. "Drew's not there."

"We're going to find him, Molly." Mal had laid his hand on his chest. "I promise you. We will bring him home."

"I know," she had said, and sent him on his way with a large tin of orange cranberry tea bread slices and frosted sugar cookies.

Now, she relished the fact that even though the store itself hummed with activity, her little corner of it was quiet and still. The scents of gingerbread and tea filled the air. Even with both the boys in her life off who knew where, Molly was content for the moment.

This is what life should be, she thought.

Aunt Margie slipped her head around the kitchen door. "You have a visitor." she said, and Molly paused in her rolling. "Would you like me to send him in?"

She never asks that. I wonder who it is. "I guess so," she said, putting the rolling pin aside and picking up her cookie cutter. "The kitchen is open to everyone, Aunt Margie." Then she grinned. "Unless you think I need a chaperone?"

"You might, with this one." Aunt Margie ducked back out before Molly could respond.

Oh really?

Molly began cutting out gingerbread men, wondering who or what might be coming through her door. Aunt Margie usually took everything so calmly, up to and including the centaurs who came in half-naked to do their holiday shopping. For her to be flustered (and she had been, or she wouldn't have checked with Molly before sending this person in), was very unusual.

Then again, when the...man...swept through her door (and swept was really the only word Molly could use to describe his entrance), she could understand her aunt's consternation. She gaped at him, her cookie cutter dropping from one hand forgotten onto the island, her only coherent thought disappointment that Schrodinger wasn't there. The CrossCat would have been thrilled beyond belief.

"Have we met?" she asked finally, bemused. Usually it was only her friends that actually came into the kitchen. Then again, there were few people who lived in the Cove that she didn't think of as at least casual friends. It was that kind of town.

This was someone she'd never seen before. She was quite sure of that.

He was tall, taller than Drew, and well-built, with long dark hair pulled back into an artfully mussed ponytail. A long, dark mustache flowed into his black beard, and his dark eyes were lined with lashes that Lai would be jealous of. Snow dusted his burgundy and gold great coat, and he paused to wipe the soles of his knee-length black leather boots before he entered the kitchen.

"No, but not for lack of trying, my dear lady," he said, pulling his burgundy-furred hat from his head and sweeping her a flamboyant bow. "Sadly, our paths have not crossed, although I have heard tales of the magic that comes from your kitchen. This morning, however, a mutual friend asked me to stop by and deliver a present to you, and how could I say no?"

Molly's eyebrows went up. "You know Drew?"

"I do. As well as his grandmother, who sent the lad sailing with me one summer to build character." He set the hat in the crook on his arm and then offered her his other hand. "Captain Pavel Chekhov, of the fine ship *The Heart's Desire*, at your service."

"*The Heart's Desire*?" Molly let him take her hand and kiss it. "The pirate ship?"

"We prefer to be called deep-sea reassignment specialists, actually," Pavel said, winking at her as he let her hand slip through his fingers. "Pirate has such ugly connotations..." And he wiggled his dark eyebrows at her.

Molly laughed. "Drew never told me he served on a pirate ship!"

"He didn't?" Pavel looked mock-shocked. "That scoundrel. I shall have to enlighten you."

"I look forward to it," Molly said, picking up her cookie cutter again. "Can I get you a cup of tea?"

"I would love one."

"Then sit." She nodded to one of the stools. "Your hat and coat can go on the pegs. What kind of tea would you like?"

Pavel set his hat on the peg but kept his coat on as he claimed his stool. "You wouldn't happen to have a delicate green, would you?"

"I would." Molly decided not to comment on the choice, but put aside her cutter and went to get another cup from the pantry. *I need more ceramic mugs for the winter, if it's going to be this cold*, she thought absently, looking at her dwindling supply. In the warmer months, people preferred her daintier cups of china and glass, but in the winter, they wanted big ceramic and clay mugs to warm their hands. All the mugs and cups she used in the tea room were different, gathered from yard sales, second-hand shops, and estate sales, so if one broke, she wasn't worried. There had been a lot of accidents lately, it seemed, or she had someone pilfering mugs. Not that it really mattered. She made herself a mental note to check with some of the second-hand shops in the next week, to see what they had.

Then she picked up the light green tea that she'd ordered at the beginning of the month and went back out into the kitchen.

Pavel was looking at the orderly rows of gingerbread men next to him. "Drew didn't mention you were a kitchen witch."

Molly shrugged. "It's not a big deal," she said, placing the tea into the mug and pouring hot water over it. She refilled her cup at the same time. "So, you have a message from Drew for me?"

"And a gift!" He presented that first: a gift bag that he pulled from somewhere inside his coat. The ornament affixed to the outside was ruby red, with sapphire blue connector beads. The card simply said, "You need to remember to slow down once in a while, especially during this season." Inside the bag was a collection of her favorite bath salts and bath beads. Molly was touched.

"He is a good man," Pavel said, sipping his tea. "He misses you."

"You may as well give me his message too," Molly said, putting the bag with her coat.

"It's not written down." Pavel put down his mug and looked at her, the amusing flamboyance gone. "Don't go looking for Old Man Winter, Molly. You don't want to get involved in this."

Ice ran through her veins at his words, but she lifted her chin. "I know what I'm doing."

"You don't," Pavel said. "Old Man Winter is not one of those spirits who will be charmed by your baking and your smile, Molly. He's a primal force. He's not going to play your games."

"I'm not playing a game," Molly retorted, stung. "And I'm not going to sit idly by and let Drew try and save MY town." At Pavel's startled look, she nodded. "Yes, I know what's going on. And since you're in the message delivery service, Pavel, you can give one to Drew from me. I am NOT the princess he needs to rescue, and it's high time that he learns that."

Pavel sighed. "I will tell him." He didn't have to say how unhappy Drew would be do get that message.

Molly already knew. And it wasn't going to stop her.

Chapter 9
December 9

"Do you think we can still find it?" Molly asked, as she and Lai climbed out of the Land Rover. She looked over the sea of people moving around the parking lot.

Unlike Monday night, when they had been one of the few people there picking out a tree, this was a mob scene. Trees and people ebbed and flowed around the two bonfires that blazed in the darkness. Above the chatter of happy children and amused (and sometimes tired) adults, there were Christmas carols too, of course. It was all a bit overwhelming.

"We don't have to," Lai said. "Didn't you get your tree here last year?"

"No, my uncle picked it up for me," Molly said, following her friend to one of the two sheds near the bonfires. "I assumed he had to go and cut it. That's the way we had to do it before when it was Foster's."

The Foster family had run the only tree farm in Carter's Cove for as long as Molly could remember, but old Mr. Foster had fallen two years ago. Rather than trying to run the farm and care for her aging parents, Cara Foster had sold the farm to a new family in the Cove, and relocated to Florida.

"It's much easier now," Lai said, as they got into line. "I called today and told them we'd be here to pick it up tonight, so they cut it down about an hour ago, and all we need to do is pay for it."

"That's brilliant!"

It was fast, too. In twenty minutes, they were at the front of the line, handing money to Josh Lavalle, the new owner. "Hi! Molly Barrett, right?" he said cheerfully. "You picked a beautiful one."

"Schrodinger picked it out," she said. "He gets all the credit."

Josh leaned over the counter, looking for the CrossCat. "You didn't bring him today?"

Molly shook her head. "He's had a busy couple of days," she said, which wasn't a lie. "He's guarding the tree stand at home."

"Well, let me get Casey to get your tree, so you can get home to him," Josh said. "Wait over there by the fire, if you would."

They did, and in another five minutes, a young man with a shock of red hair sticking out from under his ball cap came out carrying the tree, already wrapped in a protective netting. "Do you folks have rope to tie it on?" he asked.

"Yes," Lai said, leading him over to the Land Rover. "I remembered from last year."

"Great!" he said.

Between the three of them, they got the tree settled carefully on the roof and lashed into place. Then, just as he was leaving, Casey said, "Oh wait. There's one more thing." He turned back and handed Molly a small box from his coat pocket. "Dad said this was supposed to go with the tree, but we didn't want to crush it. He found it under the tree when we went to cut it down."

Molly smiled. "Why am I not surprised?"

"What is it?" he asked.

She opened the small cardboard box and lifted out the ornament, its evergreen and silver beads glittering in the firelight. "It's a gift from a friend," she said softly. "A very determined friend."

✳✳✳

The house was lovely, and huge. Schrodinger sat down on the snow, pondering his options. He'd followed Old Man Winter's confusing scent across the Realms to this place. Now, he had to decide what he was going to do. Much as he wanted to see Drew, he didn't know if the Snow Queen's edict on Molly not being able to communicate directly with Drew extended to himself as well.

In the end, he decided against going into the house. He slunk through the bushes to the stables at the rear of the house, then stiffened. Here, the scents of Old Man Winter and Drew were joined by another smell, one that Schrodinger had only ever smelled once before, on a scroll in the Librarian's collection.

Dragon.

He slipped into the stables, wondering what he would find. Dragons were notoriously retiring, regardless of the myths, and very secretive. Why was one here? Had Drew found it? Or had Old Man Winter bribed it to come out, promising it...what? To destroy another village like the Cove? Did he promise it Drew if he couldn't convince the spirit to stop?

Hardly, although I must admit, if I was in the habit of taking servants, I could do much worse than Drew, he heard, and stiffened. *Come out, little CrossCat. I know you are there, and I promise, I will not hurt you.*

The voice was definitely female, gentle, and quiet, like Molly's when she dreamed. Cautiously, Schrodinger stepped forward into the stable proper, looking for the dragon.

She was lying in a big box stall, curled up on a pile of straw. Her rear leg was swathed in bandages, and her sapphire eyes were bright with curiosity as she looked him over. *Welcome, young CrossCat,* she said softly. *You have come a long way, judging by the smells you carry. Rest here a while, if you would like.*

Schrodinger curled up in the straw, grateful for the respite. He could sense no antagonism coming from her. *How did you know I was here?*

I could hear you, she replied, amusement threading through her mental voice. *I've very little to do here other than listen, after all.*

Ah.

They sat in silence for a couple of moments, while Schrodinger collected his thoughts and the dragon turned back to the book that was spread out before her. Then he asked, *Who are you?*

I am called Ember, the dragon replied. *Your friend Drew helped me out of a hunter's trap after Old Man Winter found me.*

Drew is a good man, Schrodinger said. *He's why I'm here.*

Yes, I know. He's spoken of you, and of Molly.

He has? Really? Schrodinger blinked.

Yes, if your name is Schrodinger, which I assume it is. He misses you and Molly very much. Ember raised her head as the stable door opened. *Will you stop in and see him today before you go?*

No, Schrodinger said, getting to his feet as Old Man Winter came through the front door of the stable. *I came to see Old Man Winter.*

The spirit stopped as he saw the CrossCat. Old Man Winter towered over Schrodinger, clad in grey, silver, and white furs. Snow danced around him, and ice frosted his long beard and mustache. "What are you doing here?" His voice rumbled harsh in the still air.

I have a message for you, Old Man Winter. Schrodinger's voice didn't waver at all. He was rather proud of that. *An invitation, in fact.*

The old man's eyebrows disappeared into his woolen hat. "What kind of invitation?"

Molly Barrett invites you to have tea with her tomorrow at CrossWinds Books' Tea Shop in Carter's Cove, Schrodinger said. *She would like to discuss some things with you.*

"Then why didn't she come here, instead of you?" Old Man Winter said.

Because she can't. She promised the Snow Queen she wouldn't go looking for Drew, and he's here with you. So she sent me. Schrodinger cocked his head. *She's a very good cook, you know. Even if you don't want to agree to her terms, you should at least come and let her feed you.*

Go, Old Man, Ember added, looking up from her book. *Her lover is away, at Christmas no less, because of you. You owe her the courtesy of at least hearing her out.*

"I don't owe her anything," Old Man Winter said sharply. "I don't owe anyone anything."

That is not true, and you know it. The dragon's voice took on a note of steel. *You will go.*

The two of them locked gazes, seemingly forgetting Schrodinger was there, and the CrossCat was glad of that. He didn't want to get between that clash of wills.

"Fine," Old Man Winter grunted finally, coming into the box stall next and kneeling next to Ember. "I'll be there tomorrow. Now go, before I lose my temper."

Schrodinger got.

✳✳✳

Drew was reading in the library when the front door slammed open and then shut again. A few minutes later, Old Man Winter stomped into the room.

"Am I supposed to be impressed, or scared?" Drew asked, not looking up from his book. "Because I'm not really into either at the moment." He'd decided that if he could keep the spirit's antagonism focused on him, it would distract from whatever Molly was trying to do.

"Your girlfriend."

Those words made him look up. "What about her?" Drew said.

"She," Old Man Winter paused, as if the words hurt him. Snow curled around him, and his beard bristled. Then he said, "She invited me to tea."

Drew sighed. "Of course she did. Well, if you don't mind some advice, don't ask for coffee and you'll be fine."

"Why not?" Old Man Winter said. He went over to the fireplace, the snow around him turning to steam in the warm air.

"Because Molly hates coffee," Drew said. "She'll throw you out faster than you can blink for asking for coffee."

"Really?" It sounded like that actually interested the old man. "That's a pretty extreme prejudice."

"She's only got a few, but they're deep," Drew said. "Her baking makes up for it."

Old Man Winter grunted. "Maybe."

"Are you going?"

"Told the CrossCat I was, in front of the dragon. I don't break my word." Old Man Winter kicked at a log. "Didn't promise I'd stay long, though."

Drew didn't respond to that; his mind was too busy coming up with what could possibly go wrong when Molly and Old Man Winter clashed. Both were stubborn.

Carter's Cove might never know what hit it.

Chapter 10
December 10

It was easy to tell when Old Man Winter entered CrossWinds Books. Molly was out in the tea room chatting with one of her regulars, her back to the front door, when it crashed open and an icy wind howled through the building. The busy hum in the bookstore stopped abruptly.

Molly finished topping off Lisa's cup, smiled down at the woman reassuringly, and then turned to the front of the tea room, where a giant of a man dressed in an array of furs and scowls stood waiting.

Schrodinger came to stand next to her as she said, "Welcome to CrossWinds Books," smiling up at him as if he were a regular customer and refusing to be intimidated by him, even as her stomach knotted. Old Man Winter was the reason Drew wasn't with her. He was the reason her town was in danger.

He was impressive enough in his wild man of the woods outfit, never mind the cold aura of winter wrapped around him, but she refused to let him see her fear. "You look cold," she continued. "Come on back into the kitchen. It's warmer there and we can talk." And then she turned and walked back to the kitchen, not bothering to see if he would follow.

There was a chance he wouldn't of course, but Molly hoped

he would. Schrodinger had told her that Old Man Winter had been faintly confused under his anger over the invitation. Confusion meant that he didn't know what she'd do next. Which gave her an edge, she told herself: a faint one, to be sure, but she'd take any advantage she could get in this situation.

As she pushed open the kitchen door, well aware of everyone's eyes upon her and Schrodinger, heavy footsteps finally echoed behind her. Molly suppressed a triumphant smile. *That's it,* she thought. *Follow me. You know you want to know what I intend to do, and this is the only way you'll find out.* She refilled the kettle in her hand and set it back on the stove to boil again, then turned to face her reluctant guest. "Please, sit down. What kind of tea would you like?"

Old Man Winter stared at her as if she were daft. "Are you serious?" he said finally, his voice rough and gravelly. He sounded like he'd spent a century gargling rock salt and broken glass.

"Yes," Molly said, as Schrodinger jumped up on to his customary stool. She put his normal mug in front of the CrossCat, an Earl Grey teabag already in it, and looked back at Old Man Winter. "If you don't like tea, I have hot chocolate, cider, or chai as well."

"No coffee?" he said, daring her.

Molly drew herself up, offended. "No. This is a TEA shop. If you want coffee, we can go to Katarina's and talk. It won't be as private there, but it's up to you."

They locked gazes, and surprisingly, it was Old Man Winter who looked away first. "Boy said you'd throw me out if I asked for it."

"Normally I would," Molly said honestly. "But I need to talk to you today, and besides, you've never been here before. That was your one warning. The next time, I will, without hesitating."

"Do you know who I am?" Old Man Winter said, drawing himself up.

"Besides the man who made it so I'm spending the Christmas season alone, wondering if my town is going to be destroyed at any moment, and if I'll ever see my boyfriend again? No, I have no idea."

The minute the words flew out of her mouth, Molly groaned inwardly. She had promised herself and Schrodinger that she wouldn't lose her temper. So much for that.

Old Man Winter stared at her and she braced herself for the explosion, or worse. What if he left? What would she do?

To her surprise, he finally sank down on the stool next to Schrodinger. "Something black. Please." The please sounded like it might have hurt him to say it.

"Coming right up." Molly went into the pantry for a large mug, and two of her special Christmas tea bags. After she'd poured hot water in all their cups, she set a tray of cookies and scones that she'd prepared especially for him in the middle of the island. "Would you like milk or sugar?"

"Not in tea," he grunted, and she mentally gave him points for that. Molly preferred her tea black as well, unless she was sick. "Now, what did you want to talk about?"

Molly sat down across from him and gathered her courage. "I want to talk to you about the deal you made with the Snow Queen."

Old Man Winter grunted. "What about it?"

So that's the way this is going to go, is it? Molly's eyes hardened. "She kidnapped Drew so that he could try to change your mind before you destroy the Cove. I don't think that's fair."

"Which part?" he asked, picking up his mug and taking a sip. Apparently he liked the flavor, because he took a second, longer pull.

"Either!" Molly said. "What gives you the right to decide to destroy the Cove and kill everyone?"

"I'm Old Man Winter," he said, as if that explained everything.

"That's horrible," Molly said. "Just because you can do something doesn't mean you should. What has the Cove done to you?"

"The Cove? Nothing. You're just a convenient target." He sipped again from his mug of tea. "It's humanity in general that has to go."

"Why? What has humanity done to you?"

Old Man Winter put his mug down and stared at her, cold fire blazing in his eyes. "Humanity is a cancer," he said quietly. "Because of humans and their wars, the Realms are in chaos. Even now, I have a friend who nearly died because a selfish, evil human hunter set an iron trap that almost severed her leg."

"So you'd condemn the entire race for the actions of one or two?" Molly said, heat rising in her cheeks. "You're no saint either, Old Man. I've been doing some research on you, and your wolves. You used to help people, but it seems like you changed. You hunt innocent people for the fun of it. What gives you the right to denounce us and continue on yourself? You're a hypocrite."

"So are most people," he said. "You're all going to die at some point, Molly. What does it matter when?"

Easy for you to say, Schrodinger said. *You're immortal. It matters a great deal to those of us who don't have that option.*

Molly ground her teeth together. "Not all humans are bad. Drew is helping you with your friend. Schrodinger said so."

"Because I dragged him along."

You needed him, Schrodinger corrected. *You can't touch iron traps. If you destroy us, who will help you in the future?*

"I won't need help if humans aren't around to leave iron traps," Old Man Winter said.

"So what, you start with the Cove and then kill everyone else?" Molly said, shuddering. "No. That won't work for me. And if you made a deal with the Snow Queen, then why not make one with me too?"

Old Man Winter looked warily at her. "I'm listening."

"Come with me to a few things around the Cove before

Christmas," Molly said. "Let me show you the people you are so bent on destroying. After all, if we're all as bad as you think, this should only stiffen your resolve, right? What's the harm?"

They looked at each other for a long, long moment, and Molly saw the wheels turning in his head. Would he agree? Or would he get up and leave? Had she ruined everything?

He finally seemed to see the tray in between them. "What are these?"

"Sugar cookies, peppermint candy cane cookies, and orange cranberry scones," Molly said. "I wasn't sure what you would like. Please, have some."

After studying the plate a bit more, Old Man Winter picked up a scone and bit into it. Molly watched his face soften just for a moment as the sweet, citrusy pastry melted in his mouth. The scone was quickly gone, and when he looked up at her again, his scowl didn't seem quite as harsh. "Good," he said grudgingly.

"I'll send you home with some," she offered. "They're one of Drew's favorites as well."

"Boy didn't mention you were a kitchen witch."

Interesting. I wonder why. "He's probably used to everyone knowing," Molly said out loud. "It's not like I keep it a secret. Try a cookie."

Old Man Winter took a brightly-frosted sugar cookie. Molly had spiked them with lemon rind and thyme, and his scowl fractured a bit more as he ate it.

Two more cookies, and I might actually see him smile, she thought. "Do we have a deal?"

He finished his tea, and took another cookie from the tray. "This is supposed to be Drew's challenge," he said finally.

"No, Drew has to convince you that there are good people left in the world," Molly said. "I just want to show you my hometown."

"Semantics," he grunted. Then he cocked his head, as if listening to something far away. "Fine, little kitchen witch. I'll come around with you and see what your town has to offer."

"Good." Molly smiled brightly at him. "Then meet me back here tomorrow night at 6 pm. And dress nicely, please."

"Why?" He looked warily at her.

"Because you're taking me to the ballet."

✳✳✳

Molly and Schrodinger cleaned up quickly that night. She was exhausted, not just from the strain of meeting Old Man Winter in the flesh, but from the interrogation from Aunt Margie afterward.

The front door had barely closed behind Old Man Winter when Aunt Margie had come barreling in to the kitchen, demanding, "What just happened? Who was that? Why was he here?"

"Old Man Winter, and he was here because I invited him," Molly had replied, setting a cup of tea in front of her aunt and refilling the cookie tray. Old Man Winter had quite the sweet tooth, it turned out. "We had a very civilized conversation, and I'm sure you'll be seeing him more in the next few weeks."

He's coming with us to the ballet, Schrodinger had said, and Aunt Margie had stared at both of them.

"You need to tell me everything," she'd said finally.

So Molly had, stressing that the reason was NOT for public consumption. "Because really, no one needs to know that he might wipe the Cove off the map," she'd said, and luckily, Aunt Margie had agreed. However, after both conversations, Molly was looking forward to a nice quiet night at home with a book, Schrodinger, and a bottle of wine.

She and Schrodinger went out the front door after calling goodbyes to Aunt Margie (who was staying late to catch up on some bookkeeping). Molly blessed the forethought that had made her pack both her gloves and her thick wool mittens; the temperature had dropped rapidly after the sun went down, and there was a bitter bite to the air. She wrapped the scarf her mother had knit her around her face and turned to head down the street.

Are you sure you're warm enough? Molly thought at Schrodinger. It was too cold to actually talk.

Yes. He was wearing the coat she'd bought him last Christmas, but he'd steadfastly refused to let her put boots on him. Schrodinger started to say something else, but then he paused, one foot lifted. *Do you hear that?*

Molly stopped and listened hard. *Bells? Are those bells?*

Those aren't St. Michael's bells, Schrodinger said, looking around.

No, they're sleigh bells! Molly looked around as well. The roads were icy enough that Doc Robbins' sleigh had no problems coming down the lane towards them. Except this wasn't Doc's sleigh.

This sleigh was drawn by two elegant black horses, decked in silver and black barding, and the young man who drove it was bundled up even more than Molly was, making his identity unknowable. As the sleigh drew alongside them, Pavel grinned down at them from the back, where he was snuggled under a massive amount of furs and blankets. "Can I interest you two in a ride?"

Molly and Schrodinger willingly climbed aboard and snuggled in with him. "Did Drew send you?" Molly asked, pulling her scarf down enough to speak. Down in the back of the sleigh, protected from the wind, it was a little warmer.

"Of course," Pavel said. "He wanted to come himself, but, well..."

"I wonder what I can get Jade to do for us to make up for this," Molly mused, and Pavel laughed.

"I don't know," he said. "I think you managed to give her quite a start today!"

"It's good for her - helps to keep her young," Molly said, and looked keenly at him. "Are you working for her too?"

Pavel laughed again. "She's always paid her bills on time," he said, and winked. "Now, why don't we get on with this tour?"

"Tour?" Molly asked.

"Yes. I haven't seen Carter's Cove in a long time. I was hoping you'd go with me."

Molly looked at Schrodinger. "We didn't have too many plans."

And we can see the lights! Let's go! The CrossCat perked up. He loved looking at the lights.

Pavel nodded, and shouted something to the driver in a language that Molly didn't recognize. The horses leapt forward.

For the next hour, they went on a tour of the entire town, looking at the Christmas lights and decorations that twinkled in the clear night air. Despite herself, Molly enjoyed it thoroughly.

When he dropped them off in front of their building, Pavel pressed a package into Molly's hands, and murmured softly, "Just be careful, Molly. Old Man Winter is not someone to be trifled with."

Molly pulled off her mitten and carefully extracted the ornament from the box. Looking at the gold and silver beads caught around the glass ball, she said, "Neither am I, Pavel. Neither am I."

✳✳✳

"She's got spirit."

Drew, who was spreading salve on Ember's wounds, shook his head. "That's one word for it, yes," he said. Once he was done with the salve, he looked up at the old man standing over him in the entrance to the stall. "Did you enjoy yourself?"

Old Man Winter grunted, and Drew noted cookie crumbs in his beard. "I asked her for coffee."

"I'm surprised you're unmarked."

"She said it was my one warning, and offered to go with me to Katarina's."

Drew considered that as he wound a fresh bandage around the dragon's leg. "That wouldn't have been too bad, actually. Katarina's almost as good a baker as Molly is, and Mick's usually good for a drop of something a bit stronger. But it's not as private."

"You didn't mention she was a kitchen witch," Old Man Winter said.

"Must have slipped my mind," Drew said, and the old man snorted.

"She sent me home with a box of stuff. It's in the fridge. I'd appreciate it if you left me some of the scones." Then Old Man Winter walked out into the night.

She's made quite an impression, I'd say, Ember said. *I would like to meet your Molly someday, I think.*

"She'd probably like to meet you too," Drew said. "I'm just wondering what she's going to do next. And what she actually asked him to do."

You could ask him.

"I might," Drew said, starting to clean up the stall. "I just might."

Chapter 11
December 11

"Wait, she said WHAT?" Drew stared at Pavel, torn between horror and admiration.

"She said that--"

"No, I heard you the first time." Drew sighed and put his palm to his forehead, wondering if maybe he could blame the entire last week on a fever dream. His skin, however, was cool. No such luck.

"I have slightly more bad news," Pavel said, and Drew groaned.

"Hit me. I think I'm ready."

"She's taking him to the ballet tonight."

"WHAT?" Drew's jaw dropped. "To Lily's ballet?"

"I guess." Pavel shrugged. "I asked her what she was doing tonight, to see if she needed anything, and she said she was taking him to the ballet. And Schrodinger told me he was plenty able to be her chaperone."

"To the ballet," Drew repeated. "She's taking Old Man Winter, who is threatening to possibly destroy her home, to the ballet." The absurdity of the image of the old spirit sitting in the auditorium, watching the ballet students move through the dance, hit him and his shoulders began to shake as he laughed.

When he was done, he looked up to see Pavel watching him.

"Are you okay?" the pirate asked.

"I don't know anymore," Drew said. He covered his face in his hands. "This could go up in flames, you know."

"It could," Pavel agreed. "Or it could not."

They sat in silence for a few minutes, each lost in their own thoughts, and then Pavel said, "Do you need me to deliver anything today?"

"Huh?" Drew looked up. "Oh, no, sorry. Thanks, Pavel. I've got the next couple of days taken care of." Drew pulled himself up from the kitchen table where they had been sitting. "Come back tomorrow night? I'll have the next gift ready for you."

"Of course." Pavel drained the rest of his beer and got up as well. "This is more fun than I've had in a long time! And she sends me home with goodies for the crew!" He grinned. "You'd better keep her close--my crew is ready to kidnap her so they can get cookies at any time!"

"Big, bad pirates, looking for cookies?" Drew laughed despite his worry. "There's an image!"

"Wouldn't you, for Molly's cookies?" Pavel joined in his laughter. "Besides, even pirates appreciate good baking!"

After Pavel left, however, dread replaced the laughter. Drew went out to check on Ember, wondering what the heck he was going to do now. Molly's proposal to Old Man Winter hadn't been designed to give her boyfriend a heart attack, he knew--but it nearly had. And now that Old Man Winter had actually accepted...He sighed and opened the stable door.

That was a very deep sigh, Ember said, lifting her head to look at him. Her sapphire eyes were kind.

"I'm worried about Molly," he admitted, crouching down to look at her leg. It had only been a few days, but whatever was in the ointment that Old Man Winter had him putting on the wound had worked miracles. The iron was almost all leached out--the pad he pulled off only had a faint red tinge on it. The wound itself was smoothing out, the flesh starting to grow back, and he could see the beginnings of scales on the edges. That, at least, was one good thing.

Your young friend Schrodinger does not seem as worried as you are, Ember said, watching him. *I wonder if she is as delicate as you seem to think.*

"Delicate? No. Out of her league? Probably." Drew smeared more ointment on the wound and laid a fresh dressing down.

Perhaps. Perhaps not. Ember stretched her neck out and tapped him almost playfully on the shoulder with her head. *Perhaps you underestimate her.*

"It's possible," Drew said. "I hope so."

✳✱✳

How do I look? Schrodinger demanded, looking over at Molly again.

"You look fine, just like you did five minutes ago," she told him, trying not to smile. "I promise you, you are handsome."

I want to look perfect for Lily! He jumped up and put his front paws on the windowsill of the bookstore again, looking at himself in the glass and admiring the bow tie he wore. Aunt Margie had done the unthinkable during the Christmas season-- she had closed the bookstore for the entire day. It was, as Schrodinger kept reminding Molly, a very important day.

And I'm bringing Old Man Winter to it, she thought, wondering if she should be worried. Everyone else seemed to be, including Schrodinger. She was excited. For the first time since she, Lai, Sue, and Noemi had been in grade school, she was going to see the Carter's Cove Dance School put on their version of *The Nutcracker*. It was made more sweet by the fact that her six-year-old niece Lily was dancing in it for the first time.

Do you think he'll really show up? Schrodinger asked, looking over his shoulder at her.

Molly was about to answer when an icy wind blew around her, nearly blinding her. As she blinked away tears, she looked up to see Old Man Winter, complete with scowl, walking down the street towards her.

"I'm so glad you came," she called out, as if she were meeting an old friend. "You're going to enjoy this."

He grunted.

"However," Molly continued, looking him up and down. "You might be a bit overdressed."

"What?" Old Man Winter said, stopping beside her and looking down at her, his white eyebrows pulling together. "What are you talking about?"

"Fur coats are a bit much for an early evening performance, even in this cold winter," Molly said, gesturing to the heavy furs he wore again. "And you'll boil when we sit down in the auditorium." She looked him up and down again, wondering if he'd fit in an auditorium seat. "Then again, I guess we could stand in the back. We won't be able to see as well, but you won't overheat as much."

He glowered at her for a long minute, and Molly stared back at him with an innocent look, giving as good as she was getting. Then that wind blasted around them again. When her eyes cleared, she saw him standing in a neat charcoal grey suit, with a tailored wool overcoat and a dark grey trilby hat. Instead of the tall walking stick he'd been carrying, he had a polished black cane. And he seemed to have shrunk--perhaps it had just been the furs making him seem immense? She didn't know. "Is this better?" he growled.

"Much." Molly beamed at him and took his arm. "Trust me, you'll be much more comfortable."

And now you can sit with us! Schrodinger added. *And see the baby!*

"Baby?" Old Man Winter said sharply. "What baby?"

"My new niece," Molly said, as they strolled down the street towards the Dance School. "She's just a few months old, and she's adorable."

"I don't do babies," Old Man Winter said.

How can you not do babies? They're so cute!!!!

Molly chuckled at that, wondering just how much experience Old Man Winter had with babies. "He's excited," she confided to the spirit, as Schrodinger danced ahead of them. "He's never been to the ballet before. I haven't the heart to tell him that it's not going to be the Met."

It's going to be amazing! Schrodinger called back. *Magical!*

There was a line, of course, and as they joined it, Molly saw and ignored the startled looks in her direction. When they came up to the ticked window, Noemi grinned at them and said, "Three tickets, Molly?" When Molly nodded, she continued, "I hope you like the performance, Mr. Winter! The kids have worked hard on this!"

Old Man Winter peered sharply at her, perhaps wondering if she was making fun of him. "We'll see," he said finally, taking the program she handed him. "We'll see."

"Noemi was the Sugar Plum Faery when we danced this," Molly told him, as they went into the auditorium.

"You danced this?" Old Man Winter said.

Molly nodded. "I was a snowflake," she admitted. "Not very graceful at all. But I had fun."

They settled into seats next to Aunt Margie and Uncle Art, and Molly reached eagerly for baby Kaylee, who cooed at her. The entire family was there to support Lily, even Jack, who thumped his tail eagerly when he saw Schrodinger. The CrossCat made a beeline for the shepherd/hound mix, who scooted over in the seat to make room for him. Molly waved to her folks and her brother and sister-in-law before settling down to make faces at her niece.

"They allow animals in here?" Old Man Winter said, surprise

in his voice.

"Why not?" Molly said, blinking. "As long as they're well-behaved, everyone is welcome. And Jack is a member of the family, just like Schrodinger." And they were far from the only non-human members of the audience.

Old Man Winter grunted. It seemed to be his most common form of communication. "What are we watching again?"

It was amazing how he managed to growl even in a whisper, she thought. *"The Nutcracker,"* she told him, and explained the general story of Clara, her uncle Drosselmeyer, and the magical Nutcracker prince who took her to Faeryland.

"And your niece is dancing in this?"

"Yes, as a snowflake." Molly grinned at Kaylee, who blew spit bubbles back at her. "I can't wait."

Kaylee looked over at Old Man Winter, who scowled at her. It didn't seem to faze her in the least; she cheerfully burbled at him. He looked away uncomfortably. "Are you going to hold her the entire time?"

"No, I should give her back," Molly said regretfully, and handed the baby back to her aunt, who passed her along the row to Corrine.

The house lights dimmed, and the stage lights came up. For the next two hours, Molly sat in rapt silence, watching the beloved ballet come to life. The snowflakes were adorable, of course, and the young girl they had as Clara was amazing. It was perfect.

And then it was over, and Lily came bolting down the aisles to throw herself into her grandparents' arms. "Did you see me?" she cried. "Did you see?"

"We did!" Mrs. Barrett said warmly. "You were the best snowflake!"

Molly bit back a giggle at that. The snowflakes had come out in a rag-taggle line, and none of them had really been on time to the music. But they had been perfect. Snow didn't fall all the same, so why should dancing snowflakes be orderly?

Then Lily saw Old Man Winter standing behind Molly and her eyes widened. "Are you...Santa Claus?" she whispered, awed.

Molly turned to look at Old Man Winter, wondering what his response would be. He was staring down at the little girl. "Well?" Molly said, when he didn't respond. "Are you?"

She half-expected him to say something angry and storm off, but he surprised her. Coming forward, he actually knelt down to Lily's level to respond. "No, child, I'm not. But I do know him."

"Are you his brother?" Lily asked, leaning in.

"Something like that." To Molly's absolute shock, Old Man Winter winked at the little girl. "Do you want me to tell him something for you?"

Lily nodded, and leaned over even farther to whisper something Molly couldn't hear into his ear.

"I'll be sure to tell him," Old Man Winter said solemnly. "You were a beautiful snowflake."

Lily beamed at him and threw her arms around him. "Thank you! You should come out with us!" Then she ran off with her mother to collect her things.

"Yes, thank you," Molly said as Old Man Winter stood up, leaning on his cane. "You just made her night."

"Harrumph," he said, but there was a softening of his features that she hadn't seen before. "No need to make her unhappy now. Life will do that soon enough." He looked after Lily. "You'll be heading out with them?"

Molly nodded. "We're taking Lily for ice cream." She paused, and said, "Would you like to join us?"

Old Man Winter actually seemed to consider it for a moment. "No," he said finally. "I think I need to head home as well. But thank you." And Molly heard the sincerity in his voice. "This was...not what I was expecting."

"There's a carol sing at the church on Thursday," Molly said, not really addressing his last comment. "You are more than welcome to join us, if you would like. I have a new book of carols."

"I might." And then he turned and melted into the crowd, disappearing from view.

Wow. Schrodinger appeared beside Molly. *I think he actually enjoyed himself.*

"I think he did too." Molly leaned down and picked Schrodinger up so he wouldn't get stepped on. Then she looked at the CrossCat. "Where did you get that?"

In his mouth was a small gift bag. *Jack and I found it,* he said. *Under the tree in the lobby. It has your name on it!*

She shifted him to one arm and reached into the bag with her free hand. The ornament was all shimmery white, just like Clara's nightgown, and attached to the top was a sterling silver charm, a tiny pair of ballet slippers. The card with the ornament said, "I hope you enjoyed the ballet. I'm sorry I missed it."

Me too, she thought, looking out the window at the night, heedless of the people surrounding her. *Me too.*

✳✳✳

As soon as he was back on the Road, Old Man Winter dismissed the suit and cane, resuming his customary furs with something akin to relief. It had been a very, very long time since he'd voluntarily sat with that many beings. He wasn't sure he'd enjoyed it at all.

But the dancing - that had brought back memories that he'd thought long dead. Even the littlest children, dancing out of cadence and clearly having the time of their lives, had touched the spark that he'd buried deep inside himself. Now, he shoved that spark back down angrily.

"Don't be a fool," he told himself, stomping down the Road. "This changes nothing."

Are you sure? Her voice floated out of the ether, slightly arch. *Now that you know some of the faces of the people you will be affecting, can you say that it changes nothing?*

"It changes NOTHING!" he roared. "If anything, it makes me want to do it sooner."

And why is that?

He saw Lily again, glowing with happiness and innocence. "Because then she won't have to grow up and lose that happiness."

That's horrible.

"That's life," he said, and stomped off.

Chapter 12
December 12

"She really asked him to do that?" Sue asked, admiration in her voice. "What did you do?"

"I thought my heart would stop," Molly admitted as she set gumdrops in the frosted wreath in front of her. The island was stacked high with gingerbread leaves: Father Christopher had ordered the wreath for the carol sing on Thursday. Molly had never made a wreath, but figured it couldn't be that hard. So she was experimenting with putting it together. "I honestly thought he was either going to holler at her or walk away completely."

"As if anyone could holler at Lily," Sue said, stealing a gumdrop from the bowl. "She's too adorable."

"Oh, she's been hollered at a few times," Molly said, admiring the effect of the red gumdrops peeking out through the iced leaves. "But not this time, luckily. He was very nice to her." She picked up the piping bag and started adding another layer of leaves. "So, what did you find out?"

Sue had dropped by on her lunch break to bring Molly the information on Old Man Winter she'd found in the museum archives. The folder wasn't very thick.

"Not a lot," Sue admitted. "There's a couple of old diary entries I made copies of for you. One is from Captain Carter's journal, so Old

Man Winter has been involved with the Cove from the start. But he hasn't been around in a long time. I think the newest reference I found to him being actually here was in the 1800s."

"So it's been a while." Molly set her icing bag aside. "That's probably why he didn't mention it. Anything else?"

"Yeah, there was a neat treatise that one of the managers of the Gate Station did in the early 1920s about Old Man Winter and where he might have originally come from." Sue pulled out the papers in question and handed them over. "He seems to have been a bit of a theoretical anthropologist in his spare time, and he did some traveling, interviewing various people about what he called 'the Old Man Winter myth.' He apparently never meet Old Man Winter in person, and was dubious about whether he actually existed."

"Really?"

Sue nodded. "It's pretty interesting reading. He ended up concluding that if Old Man Winter really did exist, he was somehow related to the Snow Queen."

"Funny that he accepted her being real, but not Old Man Winter," Molly said, flipping through the pages.

"Well, considering how she shows up every Christmas, it would be hard to deny that she existed." Sue put down the rest of the folder in a clear spot on the island, and then snagged one of the unfrosted gingerbread leaves. "And now, I need to go and grab my Chinese takeout for lunch, then head back to the mines. I'll let you know if I find out anything else!"

"Thanks," Molly said, already sinking onto her stool and reading. "See you."

She didn't move much over the next hour, except to reach for her tea cup occasionally. The stories about Old Man Winter were varied and, to her surprise, there were as many about his kindness and help as there were about his wolves and his vengeance. After she'd finished, Molly stared off into space for a bit, wondering what she could do with this information. She'd hoped it would help her understand the spirit more, but it just gave her more questions.

Old Man Winter hasn't always been a spirit of vengeance, and it seems like in the early days, it was targeted vengeance, she mused. *So what changed? Why is Jade so worried about him?* Because the Snow Queen's fear was not just for the Cove, Molly realized now. She had been equally concerned about Old Man Winter, and if he were related to her, then Molly could understand why. *So what can I do to help him realize that what he's doing now is harmful to himself as well as the Cove?*

In the end, it was the growling of her stomach that moved her. She had barely heard Sue's last comment, but the idea of Chinese food was a wonderful one. Molly grabbed her coat and her wallet, then went out into the tea room, where Schrodinger was asleep beside the wood stove.

"Hey, Schrodinger, you hungry for Chinese food?" she asked, kneeling down beside him.

One eyelid cracked open. *Do I have to move? I'm warm. And comfy.*

Molly laughed at the plaintive, sleepy question. "Not if you aren't hungry. Want me to bring you back some beef and broccoli?"

Sounds wonderful. His eye closed again and she heard a faint snore.

She stopped at the cashier's desk, where DC was reading a magazine. DC had been with her aunt for years, and Molly realized that she didn't know what DC stood for. She'd just always been DC. She couldn't imagine the store without the stocky clerk.

For the Christmas season, DC had frosted the ends of her short grey curls with green. It matched her green eyes. Molly loved it.

"Did you want something from Lucky Garden?" she asked now. "I have a craving."

"No, I don't think so," DC said after considering it for a moment. "But thank you."

Aunt Margie had gone to lunch with Uncle Art, so Molly stepped out into the chill air and headed for Lucky Garden, enjoying being out on her own for once.

Not for long, however. As she was strolling along, looking at the window displays, Father Christopher fell in beside her. "I thought it was Wednesday," he said. "Aren't you supposed to be at work?"

"Late lunch break," Molly said, grinning at him. "I had a hankering for Peking ravioli. You?"

"Stretching my legs," he said. "But now that you mention it, I believe there may be an egg drop soup calling my name."

Before long, they were ensconced in a little booth in Carter's Cove's only Chinese food restaurant with steaming cups of green tea in front of them.

"I hear you've been busy," Father Christopher said, sipping his tea.

"You mean Old Man Winter." Molly decided to cut to the chase. "I'm not going to just sit around and wait for Drew to come home, Father. You know me better than that."

"I do." He nodded. "But you know I have to caution you. Old Man Winter isn't your normal customer."

"Who is, in this town?" But Molly knew what he was saying. "I know. He's an old man with a lot of power and, for some reason, a lot of bitterness towards humans. But I think I can help Drew change his mind about us."

"Maybe. Just be careful, Molly." Father Christopher held up his hand to stop her saying anything. "And yes, I know, you think you're always careful. But you aren't. And this time, you may have bitten off more than you can chew. Even with Schrodinger's help."

"I won't know until it's over," Molly said. "And I can't stop now."

"I know." Father Christopher smiled at her. "It's part of what we love about you. And speaking of Drew..."

"Oh my goodness!" Molly said, as she accepted the red and gold stocking he pulled from his messenger bag and handed to her. "Where did he find this?"

"I have no idea," Father Christopher said. "I do know that he's been planning this December for a while, and that he's doing an amazing job of making you smile, even from a distance. We haven't seen you smile this much in the last few months."

"I haven't had reason to smile," she said, peeking inside the soft velvet stocking. She pulled out a CD with the words "Molly's Christmas Melodies" written on it, a gold and red ornament, and a red envelope. "Just wait until Christmas Eve, and Santa and I will fill this to overflowing," she read, and then sniffled.

"He misses you," Father Christopher said quietly.

"I miss him too," Molly said, putting everything back into the stocking. "I'm hoping that if I can show Old Man Winter what he's doing, maybe I can get him back sooner rather than later."

Father Christopher put a hand on hers. "If anyone can do that, Molly, it will be you."

✳✱✳

Drew was in the stable talking to Ember when Old Man Winter came in, dragging a sled behind him. The spirit didn't say anything, but he did nod to both of them before heading to the end of the row of stalls, leaving the sled in the center of the main aisle.

"Can I help you?" Drew asked as Old Man Winter came back, carrying a large sealed barrel.

Old Man Winter paused and looked at him. "Why?"

"Because I can carry just as well as you, and it's polite," Drew said evenly. "Besides, then I have an excuse to ask you how your date with my girlfriend went."

To his surprise, Old Man Winter's face creased into a smile for a minute. It looked odd on him, and disappeared so quickly that Drew wasn't even sure it had been there. "She's a spirited one, boy."

"Yes, she is." There wasn't much else he could say.

Old Man Winter looked at him measuringly, then said, "Come with me."

They moved six of the sealed barrels to the sled in total. Drew had no idea what was in them, and Old Man Winter didn't say. Then the spirit picked up the sled's lead.

"Do you need more help?" Drew asked him, opening the stable door.

"Nope. I'll be fine."

"You know, it's hard to change your mind when you're never around," Drew said, as Old Man Winter pulled the sled out into the snow.

"Perhaps you aren't the one that should be worried about it," Old Man Winter said, and walked off.

Well, well, well, Ember said from behind Drew. *I really need to meet your Molly now. That's the happiest I've seen him in a long time.*

"Seriously?" Drew turned to look at her. "That was happy?"

He smiled. Ember cocked her head at him, and he swore she was laughing. *You'd better be careful. He might decide to run off with her.*

Drew found that a horrifying concept.

✳❋✳

Had he known what was in the barrels that he'd helped load, the boy might not have been so quick to offer assistance, Old Man Winter thought, chuckling darkly. He pulled the sled down the Road towards his destination, whistling the theme from *The Nutcracker* as he trudged along.

The ballet had awakened an idea in his head as to how to take care of the people that had set the trap for Ember. He had watched the snow fall and realized that he had the perfect way to discover who was part of this plot, and why.

He came off the Road farther up from where they had found the dragon, closer to the village that he had traced the hunters to.

Ember's comment about how the whole village was not responsible had hit him, although he refused to admit it. This would let him know how deep the corruption in the village ran.

It wasn't a large village, nothing like Carter's Cove, nestled in a valley between two hills that might have been mountains once long ago. Now, they were tired lumps of earth, covered in snow, huddled up. Wisps of pale smoke hung in the air, laying low over the slate roofs. His nose picked up burning wood, roasted meats, the rank smell of manure and people packed into small spaces. He found he much preferred the salt smell of the Cove.

Old Man Winter raised one hand and clouds came rolling in at his command, dropping more snow, shrouding the valley. That meant he could place the barrels in peace.

He put the sealed barrels around the village one at a time, opening it to allow the contents to seep out. Each barrel contained a writhing mass of silvery-white bodies that oozed out, burrowing their way into the snow.

The snow snakes weren't venomous yet, but he could change that later. For now, he bade them go into the homes, into the walls, and listen.

"Tell me everything you hear," he said, and their long tongues flickered in acknowledgment before they wriggled away.

He didn't forbid them to eat. That would have been cruel, after all. And if there was human flesh in their bellies when he collected them later...well, that wasn't his problem.

Chapter 13
December 13

"Hang on, Schrodinger! You're going too fast!"

But I don't want to be late! The CrossCat went careening across the slick sidewalk, nearly wiping out as he skidded on a patch of ice. Molly (who was walking much slower and watching where she put her feet) could only watch as he tumbled headfirst into a snowbank.

"Are you okay?" she asked, making her way gingerly to him.

Yes. His mental voice was grumpy as he wiggled his way backwards out of the bank. Molly couldn't help giggling at the snow hanging from his chin and whiskers.

"I warned you," she said, taking pity on him and picking him up. He was big enough that she was thankful she'd thought to put her songbook and the tins of cookies she'd brought with her into a backpack. A shoulder bag would have been a nightmare.

But we might be late!

"Late is better than being in the hospital!"

A cold rain had fallen the night before, leaving everything coated with ice. Molly had her boots on, but even with the additional traction of ice cleats clipped to the soles, she was afraid she might slip. Especially carrying Schrodinger.

"Besides, we have to wait for Old Man Winter, remember?"

she said. "So we can't go in right away anyways."

Do you really think he'll show up?

"He came to the ballet. He was even nice to Lily." Molly did wonder if the gruff old spirit would show up again. He hadn't said he would, but she hoped he did. She had some questions for him.

They made it to the church without further incident. There, waiting on the front steps listening to the bells, was Old Man Winter, in the same suit and scowl that he'd worn to the ballet.

"Took you long enough," he grunted, as Molly reached him and set Schrodinger down on the de-iced sidewalk. "Thought you might not show."

"Sorry," she said. "Not all of us can walk on ice like it's dirt."

"Hrmph." Old Man Winter watched as she pulled the rubber and metal cleats from her boots. "Even with those?"

"Even with these," Molly said, clipping them to her backpack. Then she looked up at him and smiled. "Ready to go sing?"

"I don't sing," Old Man Winter snapped. "I'm only here to watch."

"Suit yourself." Molly and Schrodinger climbed the stairs into the church. After a moment, Old Man Winter followed them.

St. Michael's was an old church, full of dark polished wood, gleaming silver candlesticks, and the scents of beeswax and incense. Above the alter was a rosette stained glass window that sparkled in the late afternoon sun. And there were people everywhere.

Molly wove her way through the crowd towards one side of the room, not even trying to keep up with Schrodinger, who had shot off to see some of his friends. Her destination was the table on the far side of the church, where Christmas cookies and other goodies had already begun to pile up. She pulled out one of the tins in her backpack and opened it before putting it on the table, and noticed that the gingerbread wreath she'd sent over earlier with DC had been put in the middle of the spread.

"Don't worry," she said lightly to Old Man Winter, who had followed her like a cold shadow. "I've got a tin for you and Drew to enjoy later." And she handed the second tin to him.

"Trying to bribe me?" he asked, but she thought there wasn't as much bite in his tone as there had been the other day.

"Maybe," Molly said, grinning. "What would this get me?"

"What's in it?" Old Man Winter countered, the ghost of a smile on his lips.

"More of the orange thyme sugar cookies, plus lemon snowdrops and some fudge brownies." Molly had put some of Drew's favorites in the tin.

"Sounds good," Old Man Winter allowed. "What are you asking for it?"

"Information," Molly said.

The smile vanished, and he looked keenly at her. "What kind of information?"

"I have some questions about you," she said.

His face clouded over. "No."

"Why not?" Molly asked, rather surprised. "I'm just curious about some things I found. Like you've been to the Cove before, and you didn't tell me."

"Because my past is none of your business," he snapped, and then stalked out.

Molly stood and watched him go, blinking in astonishment. That was NOT the reaction she'd been expecting. *At least he took his tin,* she thought, then shrugged and went to go find Schrodinger.

The CrossCat was sitting in one of the pews with another CrossCat, one Molly didn't recognize. This Cat was regal and black, slim and yet larger half again as Schrodinger, and her eyes were a deep, dark, serene green.

Molly! Schrodinger jumped up as he caught sight of her. Then he tilted his head. *Where is...*

Molly shook her head. "He decided to leave."

Oh. Schrodinger blinked but didn't ask any other questions. *Too bad. Let me introduce you to the Librarian.*

This was the Librarian? Molly sat down next to her, and said, "It's very nice to meet you! I've heard a lot about you!"

And I am pleased to meet you. The Librarian's voice was deep and rich, much more mellow than Schrodinger's, and there was a feeling of great age and wisdom in her tone. *He is very fond of you, Molly.*

"And I'm fond of him," Molly said, stroking Schrodinger's head. "But he didn't tell me you would be here today!"

He didn't know, the Librarian said, turning to look at her great-great-grandson. *But there are all sorts of rumors going along the Roads, and I wanted to see for myself what was going on.*

Molly bit her lip, knowing the Librarian wasn't referring to the carol sing. "Unfortunately, I may have just made things worse," she said miserably, and told them what had happened.

I doubt you have done any such thing, the Librarian said after she was done. *You are curious. Young people usually are, and your request for knowledge is not anything that should cause such a reaction.* She shook her head sadly. *This is not the Old Man Winter I once knew.*

You knew Old Man Winter? Schrodinger asked.

I know many people, kitten, she said kindly. *It comes with being old.* Then she turned back to Molly. *I did not agree with the Snow Queen when she brought her plan to the Conclave, but that was not because I didn't believe that something needed to be done to help with Old Man Winter. I just did not agree with involving people without their consent. But now, I think she may have been right. We might not be able to help him, but I think you and Drew, with the help of this young scalawag, may be able to reach through the ice surrounding his heart.*

Molly was about to ask more when Father Christopher stopped by. "Molly! I see you and Schrodinger, but I thought you said..." His voice trailed away as Molly shook her head again. "Oh. Well, things do happen. I wanted to give you this, before I forgot." He held out the small ornament he was holding. This one had blue and silver netting, with a series of little silver musical notes hanging from the bottom edge.

"Thank you," she said, giving him a small smile. "It's lovely. No note this time?"

"Not this time," Father Christopher said, and he nodded to the Librarian before moving on.

Molly was about to ask the Librarian about the Conclave she'd mentioned, but the other CrossCat had turned to Schrodinger, and they were deep in a conversation. And then Sue slid in to the seat next to her, and there was no more time to wonder about what the Librarian had said.

✳✱✳

Pavel and Drew were playing cards in the kitchen when the front door slammed open and Old Man Winter, in a natty suit that looked surprisingly good on him, stomped in.

"Here," he said, tossing a tin at Drew. "Your girlfriend sends her regards."

Drew managed to catch the tin without dropping his cards or knocking over his beer, something he was rather proud of. "You're looking nice," he said. "Did you go out with her again?"

"For a little bit, yes," Old Man Winter said. "She needs to learn not to ask questions."

"Good luck with that." Drew set his cards down on the table and cracked open the tin. "Do you want some of these?"

"No," Old Man Winter said gruffly. "I'm not in the mood to be bewitched by her food."

"Your loss," Drew said, pulling out a brownie and handing the tin to Pavel. "I can't guarantee there will be any left over."

"I know where I can get more." And with that, Old Man Winter stomped out again.

Drew shook his head and chuckled, but when he looked up, Pavel's face was somber. "What?" he asked.

"If Old Man Winter is saying Molly needs to stop asking questions, then she might have pushed him too far," Pavel said, taking a cookie from the tin. "And that's not healthy for anyone."

The brownie melted in Drew's mouth, bringing him back to the Cove for a moment, and it was almost a physical pain. "He wouldn't hurt her, would he? Not Molly."

"He's Old Man Winter, Drew," Pavel reminded him. "If he had a heart, it was frozen a long time ago, and it will take more than the glow from one kitchen witch's stove to thaw that. Isn't that why you called me back? Because you were worried about her?"

"Well, yes," Drew said. "But did you see how he was dressed?"

"What about it?"

"It wasn't his furs," Drew said. "Molly's already started to change him."

"Let's hope that what she thaws out isn't worse than the frozen monster," Pavel said darkly.

Chapter 14
December 14

"Hello?" Pavel's voice rang through the courtyard. "Drew? Are you here?"

Drew stuck his head out of the front door of the stables. "I'm in here," he said. "Come on in."

The pirate sauntered through the stable doors after him. "Are you hiding in here?" he asked jokingly, and then stopped as he saw Ember. His eyes widened.

"Pavel, this is Ember, who I'm helping Old Man Winter heal," Drew said, grinning at his friend's obvious discomfort. It was one thing to know about the dragon, after all, and something else entirely to see her in her splendor. "Ember, this is Captain Pavel Chekhov, of *The Heart's Desire*, who is a good friend of mine."

Then he can't be all bad, she said, dipping her head towards him. *It is a pleasure to meet you, Captain.*

Pavel, to his credit, recovered very quickly. He swept his hat off his head and gave her a deep bow. "Hello, my lady dragon. I shouldn't be surprised to find Drew keeping you company out here, but somehow, I am." He looked at Drew. "Don't you know dragons are dangerous? Especially hurt ones. And usually cranky."

"So are you before your morning coffee," Drew pointed out. "And none of us have killed you yet."

Besides, most dragons tend to be cranky because most mortals are interested in killing us, rather than conversation, Ember said, shifting slightly so Drew could finish wrapping a new bandage on her leg, which is what he'd been doing before Pavel had shown up. *It's hard to reason with someone who wants you in pieces.*

"Points, both of you." Pavel took a seat on an old stool he found and watched. "Did you ever find out who put the trap out?"

Old Man Winter said he took care of it. I chose not to ask further.

"Probably a good plan," Pavel agreed. He looked at Drew. "So, are you hiding out here for a reason?"

"Not really hiding," Drew said, sitting back on his heels and looking at the dressing. "Old Man Winter said he had things to do, so I decided to keep Ember company for a while."

And he brought me brownies, Ember added. *I now think I might have to kidnap Molly myself.*

"Dragons who like brownies. Those are the legendary chocolate hoarders of old, yes?" Drew teased, and Ember laughed, blowing pale grey smoke into the air.

Chocolate is better than treasure anyways. What would I do with a bunch of hard, shiny stuff? Please. She shifted on the soft straw. *I will have to invite you to my cave when I am well, Drew. Show you how a real dragon lives.*

"Better watch out," Pavel warned. "I hear that's how they collect their minions."

Minions are treated very well by their dragons, Ember said.

"I'll remember that," Drew said, and sighed. "Who knows what I'll be doing when I get back? Mal might have given my job away, considering I'm AWOL during the busiest month of the year."

The Snow Queen won't let that happen, Ember said. *Trust me.*

Drew didn't say anything to that. There wasn't anything to say, after all. "I just miss home," he said, and meant it.

I know. Ember leaned down and nudged his shoulder gently. *You will be going home soon, I hope.*

He sighed. He'd looked at his calendar that morning, and realized what else he'd be missing: the wedding of two of Molly's old friends. It had been something she'd been looking forward to--and now she'd be going alone.

"Not soon enough," he said. "Pavel, are you busy tomorrow?"

"Not especially," the pirate said. "Why?"

"Want to take Molly to a wedding?"

Pavel frowned. "That depends. Am I the one getting married?"

"No," Drew said, chuckling in spite of himself. "But two of her friends are, and I don't want her to go alone."

"So take her." Pavel shrugged. "Tell Old Man Winter you have a standing commitment."

"I tried," Drew said. "I brought it up to Old Man Winter this morning, but he told me that if I was ready to give up so quickly, he'd just make up his mind now, and he wasn't feeling particularly charitable."

Stubborn old man, Ember said, blowing another puff of smoke into the air. *He's determined to prove the Snow Queen wrong for some reason. I barely recognize the man he has become, and I wish I knew why. Something happened to him.*

"Well, that's what I'm supposed to change, which means I'll be spending my day with him tomorrow, rather than dancing the night away with my lovely girlfriend," Drew said. "So I was hoping you'd squire her, Pavel. That way, she's not a third wheel with Sue and Luke."

Pavel looked at him. "I'll be happy to, but it won't make you happy. Nor Molly, I suspect."

"She'll be happier than if she has to go alone," Drew said. "Even though Schrodinger will be with her."

Pavel rubbed his beard thoughtfully. "You promised the Snow Queen you would change Old Man Winter's mind, right? And that you wouldn't contact Molly to help you with this, right?"

"Right," Drew said. "Why?"

"The big thing is that you and she aren't colluding, right?" Pavel continued.

"As far as I know, yes," Drew said, frowning. "The Snow Queen said that part of this was showing Old Man Winter that humans are honorable people who can keep a bargain. I agreed to not contact Molly."

"And you gave Molly your word that you would dance with her at this wedding, didn't you?" Pavel pressed.

"Well, of course I did," Drew said, confused. "What are you getting at, Pavel?"

Rather than answering him directly, the pirate looked at Ember. "Mistress Dragon, would you agree that the prior promise to his lady would not be overridden by a later promise extracted under duress?"

"I wasn't under duress," Drew objected, but Pavel waved his hand at him.

Ember considered the question for a moment. *I would, actually,* she said. *Promises extracted under duress are hollow at best.*

"Hollow or not, I won't endanger the Cove or Molly by breaking it," Drew said.

"And I wouldn't ask you to," Pavel said, looking slightly offended. "You're the honorable one. I'm the pirate, remember?" He looked again at Ember. "Go away, Drew. Go see if you can find something for us to have for lunch. I would like to have some words with the lady, and it's best if you weren't here to hear them."

The dragon looked at Pavel, her head cocked to one side in a way that reminded Drew of Schrodinger. *You intrigue me, Captain,* she said. *I'm listening.*

✳✳✳

Molly was baking. Again. Her dress was ready for the wedding the next day, and Aunt Margie had actually given her both Friday and Saturday off. She and Drew had planned to spend the night wrapping presents and watching Christmas movies on the TV with Schrodinger. Now, Schrodinger was watching "The Grinch Who Stole Christmas" in fascination, and Molly was listening as she mixed cranberry orange bread to include in her gift baskets. It should have been a relaxing night.

Instead, Molly's thoughts were of Drew and Old Man Winter. Pavel had told her, after much cajoling, of the house Drew was staying it and how gorgeous it was, but her mind kept conjuring images of cells and cold stone walls. Maybe it was the chill in Old Man Winter's eyes. That was enough to shiver any soul.

But he was kind to Lily. And he seemed to enjoy the ballet. Her thoughts whirled in time to the strokes of her wooden spoon in the batter. *Could I have been wrong about him? Is his soul so frozen that we won't be able to get through to him to save the Cove? And Drew?*

A sharp staccato knock on the front door broke into her thoughts. As she wiped her hands quickly on the kitchen towel near her, Schrodinger came out of the living room. *Are we expecting anyone?*

"No," Molly said, crossing to the door. "We're not."

She peeked through the spy-hole in the door, then frowned and opened it. "Pavel? What are you doing here?"

As she opened the door wider, a delicious odor spread through the apartment. "I bring dinner!" the pirate said, showing her the three large bags in his hands. "May I come in?"

I smell coconut shrimp! Schrodinger said, dancing around him excitedly. *And crab Rangoon!*

"And fried rice, and beef with broccoli, and if you don't watch out, you'll make me drop it!" Pavel told him, trying to maneuver his way to the island to put the bags down. Molly hurried to shut the door and help him by grabbing Schrodinger before the CrossCat could leap up.

"Schrodinger, seriously!" she scolded. "You'd think you haven't been fed in years!"

But it's COCONUT SHRIMP!

Pavel deposited the food safely on the island and Molly let Schrodinger go. "Drew gave me a list," Pavel said. "And I have orders to make sure I see you eat."

"Oh, trust me, I can't turn Chinese food down," Molly assured him, going to get plates. "You'll help us eat it, I hope?"

"Of course!"

She brought back plates, chopsticks, and napkins, then went back for glasses and a bottle of wine while Pavel unpacked the feast he'd brought. The smell was amazing.

They took the plates (including one for Schrodinger, who was nearly vibrating, he was so excited) into the living room, where a green monster was frozen mid-snarl on the TV. Pavel stared at it. "What is that?" he asked.

"The Grinch." Molly hit the play button and the sounds of "You're a mean one, Mr. Grinch" filled the room. They ate and watched, Pavel as fascinated as Schrodinger. Molly, who had watched the cartoon every year as she wrapped presents, found herself enjoying their reactions as they watched it for the first time. After the Grinch had carved the roast beast, she shut the TV off and said to them, "So, what did you think?"

I liked it! Schrodinger said, his voice sleepy now that he was full of Chinese food. *I knew he could be redeemed, though.*

"Oh?" Molly said, grinning. "How?"

"Yes, how?" Pavel said.

It was easy. Max stayed with him. Schrodinger yawned. *Max would have left for Whoville a long time ago if the Grinch was all bad.*

"Good point." Molly yawned too. It had been a long day, and there was still cranberry orange bread dough to be put away.

"You look tired," Pavel said. He took the plates into the kitchen, then came back and handed Molly a small box. "Drew asked me to make sure you got this, and to tell you that he's thinking of you."

She accepted the box and opened it. The cranberry red beads glowed in the light of the Christmas tree as she pulled the ball out. There were dark green beads interspersed in the red. The curl of note paper tucked into the box said, "Enjoy the wedding tomorrow. Have fun. Pavel's got something planned, I think, but he's going to take you, since I can't."

Molly looked at Pavel, her eyebrows raised. "You've got something planned for tomorrow?"

"I always have something planned," he said, and winked at her. "It's part of my nature."

"This is going to be a wedding," she warned him. "Two of my oldest friends. If you can't do something nice, I think I'd rather just go with Schrodinger."

"Trust me, Molly. I wouldn't ruin anyone's day." Pavel smiled at her. "I'm not that kind of pirate."

Chapter 15
December 15

It was, Molly thought, the perfect winter's day for a wedding. Overnight, snow had fallen in a soft white blanket that covered Carter's Cove in pristine white, like a bridal veil. She, Pavel, and Schrodinger stood with Luke, Sue, and the rest of the wedding guests outside the small woodland chapel in which her friends Mark and Charlotte had chosen to say their vows to each other. Located on the outskirts of Carter's Cove, the Chapel of the Pines was currently decked with holly, ivy, pine boughs, and silver bells. Inside, Mrs. Asher (Father Christopher's organist) was playing "White Christmas" on the pipe organ while they waited for the bride to arrive.

Molly stole a glance at Mark, looking nervously handsome in his black tuxedo, white shirt, dark green vest, and dark green bow tie. His groomsmen and the ring bearer flanked him, all dressed the same, except for the fact that Mark's vest and tie were shot through with silver. White rose corsages tied with silver ribbons adorned their coats.

"Don't they look wonderful?" she murmured to Sue, who nodded.

Then, through the last notes of the pipe organ, she heard bells. Jingle bells, attached to horses' collars. She and the rest of the crowd (many of whom had been watching Pavel, who was as fashionably dressed as ever) turned toward the field next to the chapel, where four white horses pulled a gaily-bedecked sleigh over the fresh snow. Inside the sleigh, the bride and her four bridesmaids snuggled under white fleece blankets, but Molly had to laugh at Charlotte's little niece, the flower girl, who was seated up next to the driver, waving enthusiastically to the crowd, the white ribbons woven into her dark hair flying in the wind.

The sleigh drew up to the chapel door, and the driver stopped the horses. The groomsmen stepped up one at a time to offer their arms to their chosen bridesmaid, who stepped out of the sleigh dressed in beautiful dark green and silver cloaks. Mark lifted down the flower girl, who made everyone laugh by taking a very reluctant ring bearer by the arm to drag towards the chapel.

Then Mark turned to Charlotte, still waiting in the sleigh, her wedding dress covered by a white and silver cloak, and lifted her into his arms. He set her down on the pathway to the chapel, took her chin in his hand and tilted her face up for one last sweet kiss before they entered the chapel arm in arm. Molly sniffled a little, tearing up already, and Pavel handed her a lace-edged handkerchief.

The guests followed the couple in, taking seats on either side of the small church as Charlotte and Mark made their way up the aisle to where Father Christopher stood waiting for them behind an altar decorated with more holly, ivy, and evergreen. All the bridesmaids and the flower girl carried white fur muffs instead of flowers, and all of them looked radiantly happy.

Father Christopher smiled down at Charlotte and Mark as they stepped up to the altar, and raised his arms out to welcome them. Mrs. Asher finished playing "Here Comes the Bride" just as Charlotte turned and handed her white fur muff to her maid of honor.

"Dearly beloved..."

Charlotte and Mark had chosen a short, sweet ceremony, in no small part because the Chapel in the Woods was picturesque, but not heated, and they didn't want to keep their guests in the cold for too long. Father Christopher took their vows, they exchanged rings and a kiss, and then it was over. They walked down the aisle to Mrs. Asher's rendition of "All I Want for Christmas is You" on the pipe organ and out into the air, where they climbed into the waiting sleigh.

"Come on," Sue said, tugging at Molly's sleeve. "I'm cold and need to get into the warmth of the hall."

Pavel had vanished into the crowd, so Molly was only too happy to follow her and everyone else out of the chapel. The hall was only a few hundred yards down the road, so rather then try and drive, they linked arms and strolled down, Schrodinger sticking close beside them.

"Wasn't that beautiful?" Sue said, sighing. "So romantic."

"Oh yes," Molly said. "It was perfect." *Except for the fact that Drew isn't here,* she thought privately.

Schrodinger glanced up at her but didn't say anything, and she gave him a smile. "Don't worry," she said out loud. "I'm okay."

Sue started to say something else, but then they were at the steps of the reception hall along with all the other guests, and there wasn't time. They checked their coats at the coat check and then entered into the warm hall, where they were met with cups of steaming hot cider.

"Oh, what a nice touch!" Molly said, taking two and leading Schrodinger and Sue over to their table. The cider was served in wide latte mugs, and she set one in front of the CrossCat, who huffed across it to cool it before sticking his tongue in. Charlotte had put Molly and Schrodinger with the rest of the Trio, Steve, and Luke. Molly tried very hard not to look at the one open seat.

Drew's seat, which should have been filled by Pavel, but wasn't for some reason, and sat empty throughout the meal.

Molly cradled another cup of cider in her hands at the end of the meal, trying very hard to ignore that empty chair as she watched the dancing. The hall was full of people, not only from the cove, but from several of the towns connected to the Cove by the Gates, and not all of them were human. Mark was a lawyer that specialized in inter-Realm transactions, and many of his clients had come. Charlotte was a traveling nurse practitioner for the Carter's Cove clinic, and she too had many friends from the many Realms around the Cove. *It's too bad Old Man Winter can't see this*, she thought, sipping her cider. *If this isn't a sign of how people can come together to celebrate love and life, I don't know what is.*

"You look like you're thinking far too hard for a party," a voice said in her ear, and Molly turned as Pavel slid into Drew's empty chair, looking very smug.

"It's not much of a party for me," she admitted.

He grinned and leaned over to whisper in her ear, "Why don't you take a walk outside, around to the back of the hall? You look a little flushed. I suggest some fresh air. The exercise would do you good, and who knows what you might find in these woods. Interesting wildlife, you know."

Molly looked suspiciously at him, and he winked at her before turning to Lai, who had just slid into her seat after her dance ended.

"Who's this?" Lai asked Molly.

"Captain Pavel Chekhov," Molly said, getting up. His earlier words had ignited a small candle of hope within her. "Pavel, this is my friend Lai."

"Really? A captain? Of what?" Lai turned her full attention to Pavel, who got up and bowed extravagantly to her. Molly looked around, saw Schrodinger dancing with the flower girl, and took advantage of the fact that no one was watching her to slip out the side door.

It was still cold outside, but she hadn't wanted to risk getting her jacket. Molly wrapped her arms around herself and walked carefully to the back of the hall. There was a small path there that led out into the woods. Looking down the path, she thought she saw movement.

Remembering Pavel's comment about wildlife, she started down the path, deeper into the woods. Music from the hall behind her wafted on the still air, broken only by the crunching of her feet in the new snow. About fifty yards from the hall, the path widened into a small clearing. And there, in the middle of the clearing, stood...

"Drew!"

Molly flung herself into his arms, unable to believe he was really there. But his arms tightened around her, warm and real, and his lips met hers in the sweetest kiss she'd ever tasted. It was him. He was really there.

"I've missed you so much," he murmured when the kiss finally broke. "I'm so sorry, Molly."

"Me too," Molly said, snuggling into his embrace. Then another thought hit her, and she drew back slightly, alarmed. "What are you doing here? What if Old Man Winter finds out? Or the Snow Queen?"

"He's not going to," Drew assured her, pulling her close again. "I have it on very good authority that he's been distracted for the night. And Jade said to enjoy ourselves for a bit." Molly snuggled back into his embrace, shivering slightly, and he frowned down at her. "Where is your coat?"

"In the hall. I didn't stop to grab it." Molly said, laying her cheek against his chest.

The music coming out of the hall changed from a fast dance tune to a slow song, and Molly didn't resist as Drew began to dance with her. Out in the clearing, under a dark sky that began to drop gentle snowflakes around them in a lace curtain, they danced, enjoying each other's company in silence.

One slow song segued into another, and then another. Then Drew sighed regretfully. "I've got to go, love. I can't stay longer."

"I know." Molly stepped back from him, trying not to cry or beg him to stay anyways. "I'm glad you came. I'll have to make sure Pavel is well-rewarded."

"And Ember," Drew said, grinning a bit. "She's the dragon, and she said to tell you she's especially fond of your brownies."

"I'll send Pavel home with batches," Molly promised.

"Give Schrodinger my love, and tell Mark and Charlotte congratulations for me." Drew leaned in and gave her one more hard kiss. "Stay strong, Molly. We'll convince him."

"And you'll be home for Christmas, right?" Molly asked, catching hold of his shirt. "Promise?"

"If I have to have Pavel kidnap you and Schrodinger from your parents' house, we'll be together for Christmas," Drew said, grinning. "I promise."

"I'm going to hold you to that."

She watched as he strode off through the woods, heading back to the Snow Queen's cottage and Old Man Winter. He turned back once and waved, then vanished into the falling snow.

Then Molly slowly retraced her steps back to the hall.

Pavel and Lai were both gone, to her intense amusement, but Schrodinger was there, sitting in his seat and radiating concern. There was a small box on her dessert plate as well.

Where did you go? Without your coat? He looked over at her. *Aren't you cold?*

"Yes, but I needed some air," Molly replied, sitting down and flagging down one of the waiters, who came over with another steaming cup of cider. "That's all." She picked up the box and opened the top

Schrodinger leaned over to look at the ornament, then sniffed her and looked up, his eyes wide.

"Not a word," she warned him, taking the little silver and white ball from the box. "I mean it, Schrodinger. I went for a walk. That was it."

There was no note with the ball. There didn't need to be.

✳✱✳

"Are you sure you needed to do this TODAY?" Old Man Winter grumbled, looking down at the dragon snuggled next to him on the sledge.

Why not? Ember asked him. *You didn't have any plans for today. You said so yourself. And I'm BORED.*

"Heaven forbid you should be bored," Old Man Winter said acidly. "You could have asked Drew to go and get this stuff for you."

No, not really, Ember said, shifting herself a bit. *He's never been to my cave, and despite the fact that I consider him a friend, I don't want him to be in my home when I'm not there. And he can't exactly drive your sledge by himself. Besides, I'm not exactly sure where everything is.*

"You're just trying to keep me from going to the Cove, aren't you?" Old Man Winter said suddenly, looking down on her. "What's going on there that I can't see? Is it that wedding?"

Haven't a clue, Ember said tartly. *I've never been there, and it's not as if I have all-seeing eyes or something like that. Drew mentioned a wedding, but that's all I know. You're getting paranoid, Old Man.*

"Rightly," he muttered, but he turned back to steering the sledge.

Ember lived in a cave, as most dragons did, but rather than it being a cold, dark, dank place, her cave was carved out of granite and marble, and was brightened by magical lights that glowed to life as she limped across the threshold. Old Man Winter followed her into the main room, a large cavern carpeted with pale blue moss that deadened his footsteps. He settled into a chair and watched her as she began to gather things.

Now, how long do you think I'll be recovering before I can come back? She turned to look at him.

"Probably another two to three weeks. You're healing well, but I'd rather not have you here on your own yet."

I can't see why, she said. *It's not like the hunters can come back from the dead to bother me, is it?*

"Because you can't change your dressings on your own yet," he snapped. "And what makes you think I killed them?"

I know you, Old Man. You've lost any compassion you had before, for some reason. Those hunters and their village are dead.

The sorrow in her voice made him angry. "I'm sorry, but people who try and take my friends' legs don't stir a lot of compassion in me."

So you destroy an entire village, children and all, because of the actions of what? Two people? Smoke curled up from behind a bookcase in the corner of the room. *That's a bit of overkill, don't you think?*

He squirmed a bit at that, but said, "It was a message."

Hard to deliver a message to dead people. She reappeared from around the bookcase, a satchel around her neck. *I'm ready. Are you?*

Chapter 16
December 16

*O*h my. Ember looked at the box of brownies with delighted astonishment. *Oh my. Just for a few hours?*

"I know," Pavel said, leaning back against the pile of hay. "I think next time, we should hold out for more."

Hopefully there will not be a next time, she said reprovingly, leaning down to take a brownie from the box. *I'm not sure, but I think he may be thawing. I hope so.*

"Do you know what happened?" Pavel asked. "I never thought Old Man Winter was this vindictive."

Ember chewed on the brownie before answering. *He went away for a very long time, and when he came back, there was ice instead of compassion. And no, before you ask, I don't know where he went. The last thing he said to me was that he was going to look up an old friend.*

"An old friend, eh?" Pavel rubbed his beard thoughtfully. "Interesting."

Oh? What do you know, pirate? Ember asked him, fixing her sapphire stare on him.

"Many things," he said. "And most don't have any bearing on this situation. But I have heard that there has been something moving along the Roads in these past few years. Something old. Something not seen in a very long time."

She cocked her head. *Continue.*

"Have you ever heard of the legend of the Eidolons?"

Her breath hissed out. *I have. Are you suggesting he has been taken over by an Eidolon?*

"Maybe," Pavel said. "I'm not certain, which is why I've said nothing. But I've heard stories, these past few years. And if those stories are true..." His voice trailed off.

Then this is much, much bigger than just Old Man Winter, Ember finished for him. *This could affect the entire Conclave. And it makes sense, especially why Jade thought Molly could help fix him.*

"So this was aimed at Molly. I thought so."

Of course it was, Ember said, looking at her satchel, which was now hanging on a nail in the stall. The flap opened and a scroll of parchment came out, followed by a pen. *Are you available to head to the Cove today, Captain?*

"I can, yes," Pavel said, getting up. He snagged one more brownie. "Should we tell Drew?"

No, not yet. Let's keep this to ourselves. If it is an Eidolon, the fewer people who know, the better. But Molly should know that she cannot give up now. Ember sighed. *Here, take this before the Old Man...*

"Before the Old Man does what?" a harsh voice interrupted her, and Pavel turned to see Old Man Winter standing before them, his eyes suspicious.

Before you go off to the Cove to see Molly, Ember said, nonplussed. *And I'm glad you're here. I need to talk to you.*

"About what?" Old Man Winter gave Pavel a keen look. "What are you doing here, Captain Chekhov?"

Running a message for me, Ember said. She nudged the note, now neatly folded. *Here, Captain. I appreciate it.*

Aware that this was a dismissal, Pavel sketched her a quick bow and got out. He wasn't sure he wanted to be around for this conversation anyways.

He ducked into the cottage to see if Drew had anything for

Molly, but the tech was actually napping, and looked so peaceful that Pavel was loathe to wake him. Instead, the pirate let himself out quietly, and walked down to the Gate to head to his ship, and then to Carter's Cove.

He'd hoped he was wrong, that the rumors of the Eidolons might just be that: rumors. But if they weren't--well, Molly's special gifts might be more important than any of them knew.

✳✱✳

"So, wait, Drew was out there?" Sue exclaimed. "How romantic!"

"How dangerous, you mean," Noemi corrected her. "If Old Man Winter had found out..."

"He didn't, though," Molly said, not looking up from the tray she was filling with cookies. "And that's all that matters, in the end. Now, if you guys would put these out on the tables upstairs, I'll bring up the box of mugs for the hot drinks."

Sue, Noemi, and Lai (who hadn't answered any questions about where she and Pavel had vanished to, but the blush on her cheeks had spoken volumes) all grabbed trays and headed out, while Molly went into the pantry. She made sure the box held just mugs, no saucers; there were plates upstairs already for the goodies. Then she brought it back out into the main kitchen and nearly ran into Old Man Winter.

"Oh, I'm so sorry!" Molly cried as they both stumbled backwards. She put the box on the island and rushed over to him. "Are you okay?"

"I'm fine, I'm fine," Old Man Winter said, getting his feet back underneath him. "I should be the one apologizing, not you."

"I almost ran you over," Molly said, offering him a hand. "I'm sorry, I didn't hear you come in." Then his words registered. "Wait, why do you need to apologize to me?"

"I was very rude to you the other day," Old Man Winter said.

"You have every right to ask me questions about myself, and I was rude about it. That was pointed out to me earlier, and the person pointing it out was right." He set his jaw and said, "I'm sorry."

Molly looked at him. He wasn't in the dark grey suit he'd worn before, but in something that looked rather Russian in flavor. Not the furs he'd been wearing when he first came to the Cove, but something similar, just more polished. And his beard had been trimmed, she noted.

"Well, I'm glad you're here today," she said. "And I accept your apology. Would you like some tea?"

"I would love some." Old Man Winter looked faintly hopeful. "And maybe some cookies?"

Molly laughed. "Certainly! Let me just bring these upstairs and I'll be happy to get you both tea and cookies."

"What is going on upstairs?" Old Man Winter asked, and Molly heard the faint interest in his voice. Something had changed in him, she realized. But what?

"CrossWinds Books hosts the Christmas Choir every year," Molly said, picking up the box again. "Father Christopher has an amazing choir, and we provide the food and drink."

"May I come up and listen?" Old Man Winter said.

"Of course." Molly led him out of the kitchen and upstairs to the large second floor, where the choir was setting up.

This year, as last year, the crown jewel of the choir was Starsha. The lovely Mareesh girl had grown more confident in the year she'd spent studying in the Cove; instead of hiding next to Father Christopher, she was chatting with Lai and Noemi as they set up the trays of cookies on the food table.

"Here are the mugs!" Molly said, setting the box down next to the three large drink coolers. She made sure all three were labeled correctly (hot cider, hot water, and cold water) and that the tea and hot chocolate boxes were full. Then she turned to Starsha. "It's so good to see you again!"

"And you," Starsha said, but her huge eyes with their peculiar star-shaped irises were focused on a point over Molly's right shoulder, where Old Man Winter was looking at the spread of baked goods with something suspiciously akin to glee. Molly couldn't be sure, because her back was turned to him, but she could hear the pleased murmurs coming from him.

That didn't seem to reassure Starsha, though. "Is that who I think it is?" she whispered to Molly.

"Old Man Winter, yes," Molly confirmed. "In the flesh."

"Is he here to choose his sacrifice for the solstice?" Starsha asked, fear creeping into her voice.

"What? No!" Molly said. "He's here for some tea, that's all. He does that from time to time."

Starsha's eyes widened. "You are...friends? With Old Man Winter?"

"I don't know that I'd go that far," Molly said. "But he does seem to like my tea."

"Indeed," Old Man Winter rumbled from behind them, and Starsha's eyes widened even further. "And her cookies. I must admit, I might be addicted to Molly's cookies."

"You wouldn't be the first," Lai said, winking at him saucily. "I hear the United Nations is considering labeling them deadly weapons."

Molly stuck her tongue out at Lai. "You only say that because you want more of them to yourself."

"Darn right." Lai grinned, unrepentant. "Did it work?"

"No," Molly said, and Lai's grin turned into a pout. "That won't work either." She turned to Old Man Winter, who had a mug in his hand and was leafing through the tea box. "Would you like a suggestion?"

His face was thoughtful. "Please. I'm looking for a good robust black today."

She picked out one of the Assam teas she liked. "This one will fit that bill. Or did you want a flavored tea?"

"No, just straight black. Although I might add some honey." He took the tea bag and added it to his hot water, and then selected three of her orange-thyme sugar cookies. "Thank you."

The words sounded less forced than they had before. Molly wondered what had happened to him since Thursday, but she certainly wasn't going to upset things by asking him now. "You might want to find a seat," she suggested instead. "They're going to start soon."

"Won't you be sitting? I'll join you," he said, but she shook her head.

"No, I need to make sure everything stays stocked, but you could go sit with Schrodinger." Molly nodded towards the CrossCat, who was curled up in one of the armchairs. "I'm sure he'd share."

Schrodinger looked up at her mental touch, and nodded. *Come and join me,* he called to Old Man Winter.

Molly moved to the back side of the tables as the choir gathered near the fireplace.

She loved it when the Christmas Choir came to sing at CrossWinds Books. Besides the star-eyed Mareesh girl, Father Christopher's choir this year included singers from several of the Realms that were connected to Carter's Cove by the Gates. Standing with Starsha and several of the townsfolk were a couple of wood elves with their long, bark-brown hair and skin; an older centaur who came in every two weeks to get more books and tea; and one bewhiskered dwarf with a resonant baritone that Molly remembered from a few years ago, leaning on an old, gnarled cane.

As Father Christopher stood to one side and cleared his throat, she saw Pavel come up to the top of the stairs. She waved to him, and to her surprise, he motioned her over to him.

She shook her head, but he frowned and waved her over again, so Molly picked her way through the back of the crowd, trying to stay quiet as the choir began to sing.

"What is it?" she murmured as she got close to him. "I have to stay up here."

"No, you need to come down and read this message," Pavel told her quietly. "Let the tables be for a bit. Trust me, Molly. This is important."

Intrigued and slightly worried by his demeanor, Molly followed him down the stairs.

"Here," he said, once they were in the kitchen. "Ember said you needed to read this. Old Man Winter beat me here, sadly. I thought I'd have longer before he arrived."

Molly unrolled the parchment and read.

Dear Molly, I hope this finds you well. Than you for the brownies. As I ate them, I realized why the Snow Queen had chosen you to help us.

"What does she mean?" Molly asked Pavel, lowering the note. "Chosen me? I thought she chose Drew."

"She chose Drew because of you," Pavel said impatiently. "Keep reading."

Old Man Winter has been my friend for a very long time, but for the past several years, I no longer recognized the person he had become. A coffin of anger and hate had encased him, one that I have begun to finally see melt, because of you.

Please do not give up on him, Molly. Ply him with your baked goods and tea that are infused with the love you hold for your community and your Drew. Show him the good that is still within this world, the good that you embody. If Pavel is right, and I am afraid he is, your gifts may be the only thing that can save him.

Ember.

"I don't understand," Molly said, frowning. "Is Old Man Winter bewitched?"

"I think it's something like that, yes," Pavel said somberly. "We're not really sure what happened, but somehow he ran across something that is using him now for its own purpose."

"But how can my gifts combat that?" Molly asked. "I'm just a kitchen witch."

Instead of answering her directly, Pavel said, "Have you ever heard of the legend of the Eidolon, Molly?"

She shook her head.

Pavel sighed and ran his hand over his beard. "I don't know all the details of the legend, but from what I understand, the Eidolon are the embodiment of certain emotions."

"Like love?"

"Love, anger, hate, misery, loneliness. All the emotions supposedly have an Eidolon."

"And you think he ran afoul of a negative one," Molly said, looking back at Ember's note. "And that my baking can defeat it? How?"

"How do you fight anger or hate?" Pavel asked her. "I've always been taught that it's with love and understanding. And your food is love."

"If you say so." Molly couldn't keep the doubt out of her voice. "I think you're all overestimating me."

"Which is why you're the best one to do this," Pavel said. He hugged her and then, as quickly as he'd come, he was gone, leaving her standing in the kitchen alone.

After a few minutes, she put Ember's note in her bag, and brought another tin of cookies upstairs. She still didn't quite understand what the Snow Queen and Ember thought she could do, but if it required baking...well, that she could do.

For the next hour, Molly listed to the choir sing as she kept the drink carafes full and the trays covered with sweet treats. She watched Old Man Winter as well; he lounged in the arm chair with Schrodinger curled on his lap, sipping his tea and chewing on cookies, not smiling, but not scowling either. He looked... content.

After the music ended, Father Christopher came over to the table and accepted a cup of tea from Molly. "So, that's him, huh?"

he asked quietly, nodding towards Old Man Winter, who was talking to Pertwee, the centaur.

"Yes," Molly said in an equally low voice. "That's Old Man Winter."

"Well, I hope he enjoyed the concert," Father Christopher said.

"I think he did," Molly said, handing him a plate of cookies. "He seemed to."

"Good. Oh, I almost forgot!" Dipping into his pocket, Father Christopher handed her a lovely dark blue ornament, with sparkling silver beads punctuating the blue netting. "Hopefully, Drew will be home soon to give you these himself."

"I hope so too," Molly said, cradling the ornament in her hands and looking at Old Man Winter again. "I hope so."

Chapter 17
December 17

"Excuse me?" Drew blinked, not sure he was hearing what he'd thought he'd just heard. He looked over at the doorway to the library, where Old Man Winter stood waiting for an answer. "What did you just ask?"

"I asked you who was delivering Molly's ornament today," Old Man Winter grumbled, but his voice lacked some of its normal bite. "Clean your ears out."

"How did you know about the ornaments?" Drew asked.

Old Man Winter sighed. "Did you think I wouldn't know what you were doing?" he said. "Honestly, boy, I'm old and cranky, not dead. I have eyes. Did you think I wouldn't see what you were doing? You're sending Christmas ornaments to Molly, one each day. I don't know why, but you are. So who is giving her today's ornament?"

"Luke is," Drew said. "From the Station. He's a tech."

"What is today's surprise?" Old Man Winter said.

"Lunch at work." This was going way too fast for Drew to follow. Even if Ember was right, and Molly's baking was melting the old spirit's heart (and really, that wasn't that outrageous an idea), this was weird. "Luke's bringing her and Schrodinger pizza from Giovanni's, because she loves it but never orders it."

"I haven't had pizza in years," Old Man Winter mused, a faraway look in his eyes. "What's her favorite kind?"

"Barbecue chicken, with fresh mozzarella, spinach, and broccoli," Drew said. "And Schrodinger loves pepperoni, bacon, cheddar cheese, and cranberries."

"Cranberries?"

"He's weird like that," Drew said, grinning despite himself. "You get used to it after a while."

Old Man Winter grunted. "I guess." He turned to go, and then paused and looked back at Drew. "Call your friend Luke."

"Why?"

"Tell him I'm taking Molly lunch, and to have the ornament ready. I'll pick it up at the Station. I assume he's there?" Old Man Winter didn't wait for him to answer, but walked out.

Drew sat there for a good five minutes, staring down at the blinking cursor on the computer screen in front of him, wondering what had just happened. He'd been about to email Father Christopher when Old Man Winter had interrupted him.

Then Drew shook himself and pulled up a new window. Luke had the morning shift, and he needed to catch him before he left for Giovanni's. *Or before Old Man Winter shows up and scares the crap out of him...* He tapped a few keys and logged into the Gate Station's instant messenger program.

Luke's icon jumped into view, and Drew typed, "Hey dude, you there?"

"Yes, for the moment," Luke typed back. "Going to head out to Giovanni's soon."

"Did you order the pizza yet?" Drew typed.

"Not yet."

"Head's up: Old Man Winter is heading your way." Drew paused, wondering how to phrase the next sentence. "He's decided he wants to take the ornament to Molly along with lunch."

"Are you okay with that?"

As if I had a choice. "It should be fine. In a way, it's a good thing. Says he's warming up to Molly. Just be aware that he's headed your way. Give him the ornament, and order the pizza for him." The thought of Old Man Winter trying to pay for the pizza was both amusing and frightening. Did he have money? "Put the pizza on my tab. Giovanni knows I'm good for it. Actually, you might want to go along with him."

"What could possibly go wrong?" Luke typed back. "Don't worry, I'll shepherd him through the town and make sure he doesn't destroy anything." There was a pause, and then more words spilled across the screen. "He's here. Don't be surprised if Mal sends you a cranky email later about him showing up without notice."

"I had no idea he could move that fast!" Drew typed, but Luke's icon was gone. He stared at the blinking cursor and hoped it worked out okay. *Of course it will. Like he said, what could possibly go wrong?*

His brain, ever helpful, began to provide answers to that question almost before the thought was fully formed.

✳✲✳

Molly was coming down the stairs from the second floor when she paused, inhaling deeply. The normal scents coming from her kitchen were both sweet and savory, depending on the day's baking, this...this was something else entirely. Something that made her mouth water.

"Who is the wonderful person who brought us pizza?" she demanded, swinging into the kitchen. Then she stopped, eyes widening in surprise.

There was pizza--her favorite pizza, her nose informed her. There was Schrodinger, sitting on his stool with his own favorite pizza in front of him. But instead of one of the Gate techs or the

Trio, whom she'd been expecting, Old Man Winter sat on one of the other stools, wearing a lumberjack's plaid shirt, his beard combed and neatly trimmed.

He brought us lunch! Schrodinger said happily.

"I asked Drew what your favorite lunch was," Old Man Winter said. There was just a hint of a smile (a smile?) on his face. "When he mentioned pizza, well--I haven't had pizza in a very long time."

Molly walked over to the stove and put the kettle she was carrying onto a burner. "No one delivers to your place, huh?" she asked lightly.

"No, sadly. I might have to find a place, though." Old Man Winter handed her a paper plate with two slices of pizza on it. "I wonder if this Giovanni would. He seemed very nice."

"He delivers to the mines," Molly said, sinking onto a stool. "Every week. So I'm sure he'd deliver to you." *Unless you destroy the Gate, of course,* her mind added, but her mouth was too full of pizza to say anything.

"Does he now?" Old Man Winter chewed thoughtfully on his own slice of pizza (a piece from Schrodinger's pie, Molly noticed, and wondered if it was a non-human thing). "He gave me a menu. I think I shall keep it."

Dozens of questions flashed through Molly's head at that, the primary two being how would he order the pizza, and how would he pay for it? How had he paid for this?

"I have to ask," she said, once her mouth was empty. "How did you pay for this?"

"Drew's tab," Old Man Winter said. "I offered to pay for it, but Giovanni said it was taken care of."

"Drew's tab?" Molly and Schrodinger exchanged glances. "You mean you brought this for Drew?"

"Yes." Old Man Winter wiped his mouth with a napkin, then reached into his pocket. "He said you don't often take care of yourself, especially during the Christmas season, because you're so busy taking care of everyone else. And that you love pizza, but don't often order it." He handed her a small box. "And since I couldn't help but notice that he's been sending you ornaments all month, I volunteered to bring today's."

"Volunteered, huh?" Molly said wryly, putting her pizza slice down and opening the small box, wondering who he'd pre-empted in Drew's schedule. Inside the tissue paper nestled a beautiful orange ball with silver beads glinting in the light. She pulled out the ornament and the little red envelope next to it.

"May I see it?" Old Man Winter asked.

"Of course." She passed over the ornament and then opened the envelope.

Take some time to take care of yourself this week, in addition to taking care of everyone else, the card read. *And don't forget to eat! Drew.*

"It's beautiful." Old Man Winter handed the ornament back to her. "Where did he get them?"

"He commissioned them from a local artist," Molly said. "To make me feel better."

"Feel better? Why?"

"It's been a rough couple of months in the Cove," Molly said, picking up her pizza slice again. "We lost a member of the Gate crew to a sudden heart attack, and, well, I don't deal well with death." She sighed. "He said he wanted to see me smile again."

"I can understand that. You have a beautiful smile."

Molly blinked. That hadn't been the answer she was expecting. "Thank you."

They ate in silence for a bit, each lost in their own thoughts, then Schrodinger announced suddenly, *I love pizza! We should have pizza every night!*

"No," Molly said. "If nothing else, I can't afford it."

We could make our own...

"No," Molly repeated, smiling in spite of herself. "Besides, if we had pizza every day, we couldn't have Chinese food. Are you willing to make that sacrifice? I'm not."

Schrodinger cocked his head, clearly considering it. Then he said, *I know! We could have Chinese pizza!*

Both Molly and Old Man Winter laughed at his delight in finding a solution. Old Man Winter's laugh was rusty, but it was real, and hearing it raised Molly's hopes. Perhaps they could indeed beat this Eidolon. "Maybe," she said to Schrodinger. "But if we did, we'd be rolling you home each night." She looked at his mostly empty pizza box meaningfully.

Not me. I'd run it all off, Schrodinger said.

"No," she said. "And that's final."

"You'd get sick of it," Old Man Winter said. "Trust me. Eat the same thing every day for a month, and you'll never want to see it again." He bit into his pizza. "Then again, if you put different things on the pizza each day, I guess it wouldn't get old as fast. But it would still get old."

"Don't give him any ideas, please." Molly finished her second slice and sighed happily. "Thank you for lunch."

"You're very welcome." Old Man Winter surveyed the remains. "And you have enough to take home for dinner, so I can report to Drew that this was a success." He stood up and stretched. "And I am not yet sick of pizza. Perhaps I shall go and bring Drew some."

"He likes pepperoni and sausage," Molly said helpfully.

Old Man Winter smiled at her. No, he grinned, and the expression didn't look out of place, and there was a spark of warmth in his pale grey eyes. Just a spark, but it was more than she'd seen before. "I guess I'm heading back to Giovanni's, then. I'm sure we can work out an option for payment." He nodded to them both and went out.

Molly and Schrodinger sat and looked at one another. *What*

happened? Schrodinger asked. *How did he change?*

"I think we changed him," Molly said, remembering Ember's note. "Or we're changing him back to the way he was. That's what the Snow Queen wanted us to do. I didn't get to tell you about Ember's note yesterday. Have you ever heard of something called an Eidolon?"

The CrossCat's eyes widened. *Only in stories. Do you think that's what changed him? An Eidolon? Of hate?*

"Maybe. Ember thinks so." Molly stared off into space. "And somehow, they think I can fix it, with cookies."

Well, if anyone can, you can. Schrodinger reached for a slice of her pizza. *After all, they're that good. I wouldn't bet against them for anything.*

✳✳✳

Drew's nose caught the scent of pizza just as the kitchen door opened, and he turned to see Old Man Winter coming in, a stack of familiar boxes in his hands. "I thought you were bringing that to Molly!" he said, blinking.

"I did." Old Man Winter put the boxes on the table. "We had a lovely lunch. Then I went back and decided to get more pizza." He beamed, obviously proud of himself. "Giovanni not only said he would be happy to deliver here, he gave me a coupon and a card that I can get points towards a free pizza!"

"And he extended you a line of credit?" Drew put the last dish into the drainboard, then dried his hands on the dish towel. "Wait, why here? Do you live here?"

"Here and there, but I have the option to stay here as long as I want," Old Man Winter said. "And he was happy to make me a tab." He put the pizza on the table, reached into his pocket, and pulled out a sparkling diamond the size of a teardrop. "I do have resources, you know."

"I didn't know," Drew said. "And I don't blame him. That

would pay his mortgage for a while." He opened the top box and took out a slice of pizza covered in sausage and pepperoni. "Molly told you what I liked, huh?"

"She did." Old Man Winter carefully pinned the menu to the cork board on the wall, and then took a slice himself. "Giovanni is a master of his craft."

"He is." Drew decided not to ask more questions, other than, "How did Molly like her surprise?"

"She enjoyed it." Old Man Winter didn't say anymore, but his face softened.

After they had finished their dinner, Drew put several slices of pizza onto a plate and brought them out to Ember. Old Man Winter had vanished into the snow, waving a hand vaguely in response to Drew's questions about when he'd be back

Do I smell sausage? The dragon's head snaked around the edge of the stall.

"You do indeed," Drew said, coming in and bringing the plate to her. "Old Man Winter brought us pizza for dinner."

He dragged a stool over to keep her company while she ate. The wound on her leg was healing well, and Drew realized he would miss it when she went back to her cave.

You will be able to come and visit me, you know, she said. *I don't intend to vanish into the mist.*

"That's good to know," Drew said, then hesitated.

You have questions.

"Always," he admitted. "What happened to Old Man Winter, Ember? Is it really Molly? How did he get so cold in the first place? The Snow Queen is a spirit of winter, and she's not that cold."

Ember was quiet for a bit, collecting her thoughts. Then she said, *I don't know when it started. He's always been a bit of a loner, off on his own for long periods of time. Eidolons work slowly, like cancer, changing someone from the inside. By the time we noticed, his soul had frozen solid.*

"What is an Eidolon? I've never heard of them before," Drew asked.

They are elemental spirits, older even than Old Man Winter or the Snow Queen, older than the most ancient of dragons, Ember said. *Some legends say they were involved in the creation of the Realms themselves. Others say they were spun out of the Great Mother's mind as she gave birth to the Realms. I've never known anyone who ever met one in its true form, although my grand-sire swore he met someone infected by one once.*

"So we really don't know about them."

No. Eidolons are like the dark matter astrophysicists talk about. We know they're there, but... She paused when he goggled at her. *What?*

"How do you know about astrophysics?" he said. "You're a dragon."

Yes. And a huge fan of Neil deGrasse Tyson, among others. I'm fascinated by astrophysics, and I count hearing him speak in person as one of the highlights of my life, Ember said.

"How did you..." And then Drew flushed. "Of course. Dragons can shapeshift. Duh."

Some can, yes. Some of us have other abilities. Are you ready to go on?

"Yes, sorry."

As I was saying, Eidolons are like dark matter, or black holes. We have a lot of circumstantial evidence for them, but no one has actually seen one.

Drew chewed on that while she bend back to her dinner. "So how do they take people over? Did it attack him?"

Think of it as an infection. Like getting a bug bite in the summer-- you don't really know which mosquito gave you malaria, do you? And does it matter, in the end? No, you just treat the disease. Ember shrugged. *Which Molly is doing quite well, from what I can see.*

"Molly takes care of everyone except herself," Drew said. "Do you think Old Man Winter knows he's been taken over by an

Eidolon?"

He does now.

"How?"

I told him. Ember looked up at him, mildly surprised. *Why?*

"What did he say?"

He denied it, but I could see the trouble in his eyes. She blew out a stream of grey-blue smoke. *I think he knew something was wrong with him, but couldn't say what. Now it has a name. And that can only help us.*

Drew got up and stretched. "Ember, do you know how many Eidolons exist?"

No one knows. I would imagine that there are as many Eidolons as there are emotions. And no, before you ask, I don't know if there are any positive Eidolons, although I imagine there must be. Perhaps they are just quieter about what they do. Ember looked at him, and he saw a glint of humor in her blue eyes. *Maybe that's why your Molly has the effect that she does. She could be the embodiment of an Eidolon.*

Drew smiled. "If there are positive Eidolons, it wouldn't surprise me. Although she'd deny it to her dying breath."

True Eidolons would, wouldn't they?

Chapter 18
December 18

"At least it's good and cold today," Molly said, as she helped Schrodinger put his coat on. "And it has been for the last week, so we don't have to worry about falling through the ice."

As if Indi would even open the skating cove if the ice wasn't safe, Schrodinger said. *And we could always ask Old Man Winter to make sure.*

"I don't think I want to ask Old Man Winter to do anything right now," Molly said. "It didn't work so well last time."

He's had more of your cookies since then, Schrodinger said. Then he saw what else Molly had pulled out of the mitten basket and started to back away. *NO! Absolutely not!*

"But it's freezing out!" Molly said. "Do you want frostbite on your paw pads?"

That's why I have fur there, Schrodinger said, holding up one of his paws and spreading it, showing her the fur between the soft pads. *I've never had a problem, and I've been outside all winter for years. I'm NOT wearing booties!*

"Jack has a set too, and he loves them," Molly coaxes.

Jack is a dog! I am a CrossCat, and we do not wear booties! I'd never live down the indignity!

Molly tried for the next five minutes to convince him to put on the woolen boots that her mother had knit him, but he categorically refused and she finally gave up, warning him, "I don't want to hear that your feet are cold!"

If my feet are cold, I'll go sit by the bonfire! Schrodinger retorted, and despite herself, Molly laughed.

"Fine, fine." She tucked the woolen booties back into the mitten basket that sat beside the front door, and grabbed her own knit mittens and her skate bag. "Are you ready to go?"

I've been ready.

She laughed again and they went out. Pavel had stopped by earlier in the day as she and Schrodinger were assembling gingerbread houses for delivery and invited them out to skate later that night. Given that she hadn't been skating yet this season, Molly had readily agreed.

Now, she and Schrodinger stepped out into a crystalline wonderland: one of those brilliant winter evenings when the air itself seemed to sparkle with ice, and the clouds hung low. The promise of more snow danced on the stiff breeze as it swirled past them, hurrying down the sidewalk towards the sea.

As they closed the main door of their apartment building, bells rang through the quiet street, announcing Pavel's arrival. Molly took one look at the sight and laughed again. This time, Pavel had really outdone himself.

The sleigh was black, drawn by a spirited black horse that tossed his head in protest as the driver pulled him to a stop in front of the building. He stamped one foot, obviously ready to run forever. The driver was in a black pea coat with a long red and green scarf wrapped tightly around his face. Pavel himself wore a black pirate's coat, trimmed in black fur and belted in black and gold, with a matching black furred hat on his head. The sleigh held piles and piles of furs and blankets, which Molly and Schrodinger burrowed into happily. Heat radiated up through the layers, and Molly realized there were warm bricks tucked into the bottom of the pile.

"Where do you keep finding these?" she asked Pavel. "You can't tell me you keep a fleet of sleighs in the Cove--I've never seen you here before this year."

"Ah, but you don't know that I haven't been here," he said, winking at her. "How often do you travel down by the harbor?"

"Often enough," she said. "Have you been here?"

"On and off," he said. "And no, I don't keep these. I have friends in the surrounding Realms who let me borrow them."

"Borrow?" she teased, and he winked at her again.

The driver shook his reins and the horse took off, happy to be moving. The bells jingled merrily as they sped along, heading out to the skating cove on the gentle Elizabeth River, named for Captain Carter's favorite granddaughter.

Indi Sarabian and her husband ran the skating area every year, and every year they improved on the site. This year, they'd strung Christmas lights through the trees lining the inlet: white snowflake lights which cast a gentle glow on the whole scene.

Oh, I like these better than the floodlights! Schrodinger said, hooking his front paws on the edge of the sleigh to boost himself up so that he could see better. *It looks like a snow globe!*

"It does!" Molly agreed, enchanted. "I hope they keep them!"

The sleigh drew up to the edge of the ice to let them out, drawing everyone's attention, and Molly giggled, knowing both Pavel and Schrodinger were enjoying their grand entrance. The pirate captain and CrossCat jumped out of the sleigh almost before it came to a stop, and Pavel pivoted elegantly in the snow to give Molly a hand down.

It was still bitterly cold, but the cove was protected from the wind by the trees. As they did every year, the Sarabians had built a big bonfire on the shore, and Schrodinger headed right over there. Molly and Pavel followed him.

There was no charge to skate, and Indi had built a small stand where she sold hot chocolate, tea, and coffee, and rented skates for those who needed them. She waved to Molly and turned to say something to the small child standing beside her. As Molly and Pavel sat on one of the logs to put their skates on, the child (Indi's daughter Kara, Molly saw) brought out an old couch cushion and set it in the snow, within the circle of warmth of the bonfire but far enough away from any stray sparks. She squealed with delight as Schrodinger hopped up on the cushion and stuck his cold nose onto her cheek in thanks.

"I see they know you here," Pavel chuckled, standing up easily on his skates.

"It's a small town. Everyone knows everyone, remember?" Molly said, standing up as well. She'd gotten new skates for Christmas last year, and she, Drew, and the others had gone skating until the ice had finally melted in the spring. But this year, there just hadn't been time, it seemed.

She'd hoped that she and Drew would have been able to go during his month off. But now, it was Pavel taking her hand and leading her out on to the ice for the first time. As they glided off into the crystal night, Molly told herself her eyes were watering because of the cold.

Just the cold.

✳✳✳

"Thought I'd find you here."

Drew didn't look up from the saddle he was polishing. "It was too hot in the house."

Old Man Winter grunted as he came further into the stable. "You could always turn the heat down."

"Or I could come out here," Drew said, continuing to rub leather oil into the saddle. He'd not seen any horses yet, but taking care of the tack had brought him back to his childhood again. And it gave him something to do. "Besides, I was talking to Ember."

Indeed. We were having quite the conversation about black holes, the dragon said. *You're welcome to join us.*

"Not interested in black holes," Old Man Winter said. "I'll just go watch Molly and Pavel myself then, if you two are busy."

The cloth fell from his hand and the saddle clattered to the floor as Drew stood up. "What?"

"Oh, that got your attention, huh?" Old Man Winter said, scowling, but Drew saw an odd twinkle in his eyes. "Put that saddle away and come with me. And be quick."

He was. Once the saddle and supplies were put away, Drew joined Old Man Winter in the main courtyard. Ember had joined them as well, to his surprised.

I want to finally see Molly, she said to them. *I've heard so much about her.*

"How are we going to see her?" Drew asked Old Man Winter. "Are we going to the skating cove?" And then something else occurred to him. "How can I see her without breaking my word to the Snow Queen?"

"You won't," Old Man Winter said. "We can't go to the Cove."

"Why not?"

"Because I've been there too much in the last couple of days," the old spirit said. "Don't want to screw the weather up too much, and I'm going back tomorrow."

Drew looked at him, puzzled.

He really IS Old Man Winter, Ember said. *If he stays in one mortal Realm for too long, it can freeze the enter area solid, and that's not usually healthy for anything living there. Why do you think he lives in the Snow Queen's Realm?*

"Oh." There really wasn't much more to say to that. Then Drew frowned. "Wait a minute. What are you doing there tomorrow?"

"None of your business," Old Man Winter said stiffly. "Now come on." And he set off across the courtyard towards what

Drew had assumed was a garden. The tech was hard-pressed to keep up with him as he pushed open the wrought iron gate and crunched through the snow.

No, not a garden. Drew saw instead that it was a box maze. Luckily, Old Man Winter seemed to know exactly where he was going, and Drew only had to keep him in sight.

Ember was waiting for them in the center of the maze, having simply flown in. She sat in the snow next to a pool of oddly unfrozen water, which was apparently Old Man Winter's destination.

"How is the water still liquid?" Drew asked, leaning over the stone edge of the pool. Old Man Winter stuck out an arm and pushed him back.

"Not water. Don't fall in."

"But what is it?" Drew said.

"Magic," Old Man Winter said.

"Obviously. Otherwise it would have frozen." Drew was beginning to regret not bringing something warmer than his flannel over shirt with him.

No, he means it's liquid magic, Ember said. *Literally.*

"You can make liquid magic?" Drew stared at the pool in fascination, cold forgotten. "What can you do with it?"

"Anything you can imagine," Old Man Winter said, dipping one finger in. "But mostly I use it to look at things these days."

Ice crystals spread from his fingertip, webbing across the pool's surface and turning it into a glassy mirror. Old Man Winter muttered something under his breath, and the mirror rippled, as if a breeze had rushed through it. Drew leaned over again, watching as the picture came in to focus.

He recognized the skating cove immediately. Indi had strung snowflake lights in the trees this year, but the bonfire was the same, and he saw Schrodinger holding court on a couch cushion in the snow near it. There were couples and clumps of people out on the ice, but Drew's gaze went unerringly to Molly and Pavel.

Molly's long dark hair was loose under her knit hat, flying behind her as she and Pavel raced around the ice. He couldn't hear anything, but he could see she was laughing, probably at whatever Pavel was saying to her as he skated backwards in front of her. Something akin to actual pain went through Drew--not jealousy, but a longing, deep and aching, as he realized again how much he missed her.

She is very pretty, Ember said, leaning over and looking as well. *But there is sadness in her, deep sadness.*

"You can see that?" Drew said.

Can't you?

He could, of course. Even as she threw back her head and laughed again at Pavel, Drew could see the tension and worry in her body language, signs that never really went away.

Old Man Winter was watching her too, a weird look on his face. It was almost wistful. "At least she's having a bit of fun. She needs not to work all the time. First time I've seen her not up to her elbows in flour."

"She likes being up to her elbows in flour," Drew said. "She even bakes on her days off."

"Kitchen witches don't have days off."

As they watched, Pavel spun her around and then stopped in the middle of the ice. Drew smiled as Pavel pulled the ornament from his coat pocket: this one was silver and blue, icy colors, and had a small skate charm for the silver charm bracelet her mother had gotten her in the spring hanging from the top. Molly's eyes went wide as she accepted the ornament.

"Pretty," Old Man Winter said, and Drew started, reminded that he wasn't alone. "Good choice."

"Thank you." Drew didn't know what else to say.

You're getting soft, Old Man, Ember teased gently. *Next thing we know, you'll be buying her a charm yourself.*

"Bah," Old Man Winter said. "I wouldn't bother. There are better ways to make her smile." He reached down again and stuck his finger into the magic, whispering under his breath.

Drew and Ember watched as tiny snowflakes began to fall on the skating rink. Molly looked up into the sky, seemingly directly at them, and smiled.

"I think she knows you're watching her," Drew said.

"Doesn't matter if she does," Old Man Winter said, but there was a pleased smile on his face, and Drew knew the statement was a lie.

✳✳✳

Old Man Winter went back to the scrying pool later that night, long after Drew had gone to bed. He'd told Drew that he normally watched things in it, but he hadn't told him that what he mostly watched was memories.

Now, he touched the surface of the magic, and the liquid swirled and darkened. Once again, he was back in the dark forest of long ago, where the ghosts of long-dead friends and enemies danced in the shadows of trees.

He watched the Road through the trees move onward, and saw himself striding along, his wolves around him. It was snowing: a dry, dusty, ashy snow that clung to everything. The emotions of the memory reached out and pulled him in.

There was blood on his clothing, in his hair and beard, in his mouth. The wolves snapped and growled, echoing the anger in their master's every step.

He'd destroyed everything in his path that day. No one was spared. No pity or compassion had touched him.

As always, one of the ghosts from the trees stepped in front of him, ready to plead for clemency for the village he knew was over the hill. Rather than a pale, remembered shade, though, this ghost was glowing with life, and she smiled at him.

Old Man Winter watched Molly hold out her hand to him, offering forgiveness, and his hand started to drift out. Something in the back of his head screamed, demanding more blood, more pain, but rather than giving in to it, as he had every other time he'd watched this memory, Old Man Winter dropped the sword in his hand, and reached out for her instead.

"It's time to stop remembering the hate," she said, in a voice that was Molly's and yet was something deeper, more resonant as well. "It's time to remember the love."

"It's hard," Old Man Winter said, and there was another scream that echoed through his head, urging him to stop, to move away.

"Yes. But I believe in you."

Chapter 19
December 19

"There, we're all set!" Molly tucked the last box of gingerbread into one of the large picnic baskets and looked around the kitchen. "Is there anything else I'm forgetting, do you think?"

"I think you're procrastinating," Sue said. She picked up one of the baskets. "Come on!"

"Okay, okay!" Molly grabbed her coat from the rack and shrugged into it. "Wait for me!"

Sue and Noemi were going to watch the tea shop while Molly and Schrodinger delivered the last of the Christmas gingerbread orders in Sue's car. The CrossCat was already waiting out front, watching the car.

Or he was supposed to be. However, when Molly and Sue got there, he wasn't anywhere to be seen.

"Schrodinger?" Molly called out both physically and mentally, setting the basket she was carrying down on the cold sidewalk. "Where are you?"

Coming.

The CrossCat's voice was...odd. Thin, as if he was very far away. Molly frowned. How could he be far away? He'd just come out with them not five minutes ago.

Don't worry, Schrodinger said, and this time, his voice was stronger. *I'll explain when we get there.*

"We?" Molly said, blinking at Sue, who was staring at her.

"What about we? Where's Schrodinger?" Sue said, and Molly realized she hadn't heard the CrossCat.

"He said he was coming back just now, but he said when WE get there," Molly said. She bit her lip. "Who would he have gone off with?"

"In this town?" Sue laughed. "I don't have time to list the names!"

"Yes, but he knows we're on a deadline," Molly said. "And why wouldn't he say who he's with? It's just weird."

"I think you're getting paranoid," Sue said, and then shivered. "I'm heading back inside."

"Thanks again for watching the tea room and for the loan of the car," Molly said, and Sue waved as she dashed back into the warmth of the store.

I don't ever remember a winter this cold, Molly thought as she waited for Schrodinger and whomever he was with to appear. *There hasn't been a ton of snow, but it's been cold.*

The thought of snow made her remember the prior night, and she smiled. The gentle fall of tiny snowflakes had come just as Pavel was giving her the ornament Drew had sent him with, and she had no doubt who had sent them. Old Man Winter was thawing. She was sure of it.

She looked at the picnic baskets on the ground next to Sue's car. *I should load these in with the others,* she though. But something else made her pause, so instead, Molly clasped her arms around her torso and looked around.

Sorry! Schrodinger's voice was abruptly a lot louder in her head, and Molly winced. *We're almost there!*

"Who's we?" she asked, but her question was pulled away by a rush of wind that raced past her. Her eyes watered and by the time she'd blinked them clear, there was a huge sledge coming down the street, pulled by...reindeer?

"You have got to be kidding me," Molly said, shaking her head as Old Man Winter, dressed in what she could only describe as a Father Christmas outfit (complete with holly twined around the hat on his head, she noted), pulled to a stop in front of her. Two massive reindeer with holly wrapped around their antlers stomped their feet and shook their heads, making the jingle bells on their trappings sound loudly in the suddenly quiet street. Molly could only imagine what the people in the surrounding buildings thought.

Schrodinger sat up next to Old Man Winter, nearly vibrating with excitement. *Won't this be awesome? So much better than the car! What better way to deliver Christmas gingerbread? Especially to Sarah! Sarah will love it!*

"Schrodinger said the other day that you could use some help delivering gingerbread," Old Man Winter said, and Molly saw the sly smile on his face. "And, well, I wasn't doing anything today..."

"And just happened to have a sledge and a couple of reindeer hanging around?" she said, trying not to smile herself.

"They needed the exercise," Old Man Winter said. "Fat reindeer are not good things."

"Of course they aren't." Molly gave up and laughed. "You look amazing."

"Do you think so?" The old man actually preened. "Thank you. Now, Schrodinger said we have a lot of gingerbread to deliver. Let's get things loaded."

They loaded the baskets from the sidewalk and the car onto the sledge, and then Molly ran back into the store quickly to give Sue her car keys.

"But how will you deliver the gingerbread?" Sue asked, confused.

"Old Man Winter," Molly said, and ran back outside before

Sue could ask her anything else.

"Let's go!" she said.

The sledge was long and wide, with an elaborately carved lip all around the body to tie the baskets onto. Old Man Winter stood at the back with Schrodinger, and Molly settled herself on a seat just in front of them and to one side. The reindeer were harnessed to the front of the sledge, and there were no reins. She guessed Old Man Winter didn't really need them.

"Where to?" he asked, and she gave him the first address.

It was amazing, traveling on the sledge. The wind whipped past them, and people all through the small town stopped and stared, as this eclipsed even what they were used to seeing. Old Man Winter actually laughed and waved as they passed children who pointed at him excitedly. Molly watched him, wondering privately if this was still the grumpy old man who had come into her tea room only ten days earlier.

At the first house on her list, she pulled the box containing a dozen gingerbread soldiers out of a basket and handed it to Old Man Winter. He took it and headed up to the door, she and Schrodinger following.

Little Aiden Miller opened the door after he knocked, and his eyes widened. "Santa?" he whispered, awestruck.

"Merry Christmas," Old Man Winter said gravely, handing him the ribbon-wrapped box. The little boy took it, never taking his gaze off the figure in front of him. In the background, Molly saw Mrs. Miller with her hand over her mouth.

"Momma, come see! Lyssa, come see! Santa is delivering cookies!" Aiden called.

"Yes, I see," Mrs. Miller said, coming forward to take the box from him before he dropped it. "But he and Molly and Schrodinger had a lot of boxes to deliver today, so please say thank you so they can go."

"Schrodinger?" Aiden's attention was instantly diverted.

Santa was cool, but Schrodinger was his buddy. "Can I go too?"

Not today, Schrodinger said, rubbing his head against the little boy's cheek. *Maybe another time.*

Aiden followed them out onto the porch and gaped at the reindeer. "Wow."

"Would you like to pet them?" Old Man Winter asked, and the boy nodded. "Then get your coat and boots, quick!"

Molly had never seen a three-year-old move that fast. Aiden and his six-year-old sister Alyssa came out into the yard and Old Man Winter lifted them up one at a time to pet the velvety noses of the reindeer. All the while, their mother was snapping pictures and Schrodinger was dancing around, providing commentary.

It was the same at every house they stopped at during the afternoon. Molly fretted a bit about how long Sue and Noemi could stay to cover the tea room, but after a quick spate of texts back and forth, Sue told her not to worry about it. Old Man Winter and Schrodinger were having a ball, and Molly surrendered, concentrating on making sure they hit everyone they were supposed to. And that the cookies were actually delivered.

The last house on the list was Sarah's, and Schrodinger was nearly in hysterics as they turned down the driveway. Jamie, his wife Ellen, and Sarah lived on a small farm on the outskirts of town; Molly had made certain that Jamie was on duty all day before she'd gone out, so his family could hide the gingerbread. As the sledge drew up to the house, Schrodinger jumped out and ran towards the door, shouting Sarah's name at the top of his lungs.

Come and see! He bounded up onto the porch and stretched up, ringing the doorbell. *Come and see, Sarah!*

Sarah herself opened the door, already in her coat and boots. "What, Schrodinger? What am I seeing?' Then she raised her face up. "I feel cold wind, colder than normal. Did you really bring Father Christmas with you, Schrodinger?"

I did! The CrossCat wiggled in excitement, and pushed

himself under her seeking hands. *Come on!*

Molly came up onto the porch after he'd led Sarah down the steps, and handed the first box of gingerbread to Ellen, who was staring at the sledge in her yard with her mouth open. "Merry Christmas," Molly said, grinning.

"I didn't believe the rumors," Ellen said. "But you really are delivering goodies with Father Christmas." When Molly looked at her curiously, she added, "It's all over Twitter and Facebook."

"I should have known," Molly said. "No wonder Sue said they were fine."

She brought the other box of gingerbread up to the house and then watched with Ellen as Old Man Winter lifted Sarah up to gently touch the reindeer. She ran her sensitive fingers over their soft muzzles, over their decorated antlers and rigging, building a picture of the scene in her head. It was hard to remember sometimes that Sarah had lost her sight when she was barely three.

"Thank you," Ellen said, as Old Man Winter set Sarah down again. "She'll never forget this."

"Thank Schrodinger," Molly said. "I was as surprised as you were when they showed up. We were supposed to use Sue's car."

"This is much better," Ellen said.

Sarah came up to Molly, her face shining. "You brought it! And you brought Father Christmas!"

"I brought the gingerbread, but Schrodinger is responsible for Father Christmas," Molly said, grinning as Sarah hugged her. "I'm glad you liked it!"

"I did! It was awesome!" Sarah pulled back and then stuck her hand into her coat pocket. "And I have something for you!" She pulled an ornament from her pocket and handed it to Molly. "Drew asked me to give you this."

"I would love to know how he's getting these out and about," Molly said, examining the ornament. Today's was caramel brown in color, with bright red and green beads at the junctions.

"What colors is it?" Sarah asked.

"It's the same color as gingerbread," Molly said. "Just like the houses I made."

"That's so cool," Sarah said, and grinned. "Thank you for making the gingerbread for us!"

"You're very welcome!" Molly said, and she and Schrodinger headed back to the sledge, where Old Man Winter was waiting for them.

He called out, "Merry Christmas!" to Sarah and her mother, then the reindeer leapt forward, bells jingling.

When they pulled up in front of the bookstore, Molly told Old Man Winter, "Please, wait here, just a minute!" She ran into the store, grabbed the box she'd left on the island in the kitchen, and ran out again.

He looked surprised as she handed it to him. "What is this?"

"Merry Christmas," Molly said, smiling. "And thank you for an amazing afternoon. I thought you might like to have some of your own."

Old Man Winter opened the box. Inside was a gingerbread cottage, iced and decorated to look like an old New England home in a snowy setting. Along the edges were gingerbread men, iced as well. He closed the box and stowed it under the front seat of the sledge, then turned to her. To Molly shock, there were tears in his eyes.

"Thank you," he said, and then, before she could respond, he slapped the side of the sledge. She stepped back as the reindeer took off down the street.

At the end of the block, they vanished into a cloud of snow.

✳✳✳

When he came back to the cottage, Old Man Winter unharnessed the reindeer, cleaned them up, and turned them loose to join the herd that wandered the hills nearby. They lipped up the sugar cubes he gave them, nuzzled his face gently, and then took off.

He dragged the sledge behind the stable, not wanting to speak to anyone yet. Then he took the box with the gingerbread in it into the box maze. Snow was falling around him, veiling his movements, and as he walked, he looked at the tiny cottage Molly had given him.

It was a marvel of sugar and cookie dough, scenting the air around him with its spicy fragrance. The cottage itself was very simply put together--just one room, a peaked roof, and a chimney. But the decorations...those were far from simple.

She had piped on individual shingles (and how long had that taken her?), and then frosted powdered sugar snow on top of it. Delicate spun sugar "smoke" drifted from the stone chimney. There were wreathes on every window, all of icing, and tiny lights of icing hung from the eaves. The cottage sat amid marshmallow "snow" and nestled within it, besides the gingerbread soldiers who marched solidly around the edges of the plot, were decorated Christmas trees.

When he reached the center of the maze, Old Man Winter did not go to the pool of liquid magic that he'd watched Molly in before. Instead, he sat down on a snow-covered bench and continued to study the house, lost in thought.

You're thinking awfully hard, Old Man. Her light voice wove into his mind. *I heard you all the way across the Realms.*

You knew she was a kitchen witch. It wasn't an accusation, although he'd thought he'd meant it to be.

Of course. I've seen her every year at the Ball. A burbling laugh danced across their link. *Had I realized that would be what it took to bring you back, I would have introduced you years ago.*

I'm not sure it would have worked years ago, he said. *I still had to recognize it myself, and that takes time.*

Has it worked?

It's working. Old Man Winter touched one of the shingles with a light fingertip. *But slowly. So slowly.*

Lakes don't freeze overnight, and neither do hearts, she reminded him. *You taught me that. Both take time to melt as well.*

He raised his eyes to the uncaring sky. *Does she have that time?*

That I can't answer, she said, after a long minute. *Only you can.*

Chapter 20
December 20

*D*rew? *Do you know where Old Man Winter is?*

Drew paused, thinking hard. "No, I haven't seen him this morning," he said finally. "Why?"

Can you come out here?

"Of course." He'd not heard that amount of concern in Ember's voice before, and hoped she hadn't re-injured her leg. "Let me just throw a coat on, and I'll be out."

He'd been sitting at the computer in the library, going over his Facebook feed and looking at all the pictures from yesterday. There were a ton of them, each with the same elements: Old Man Winter, dressed as Father Christmas, holding various small children up to pet two enormous reindeer, a gentle smile on his face. Now, as he shrugged into his coat, Drew wondered just what kind of magic Molly had been weaving into the cookies and scones she'd fed the old man.

And how much of it he'd eaten as well...

Ember wasn't in the stable, as he'd thought--she was in the courtyard, stretching out her wings in the brisk air. Drew stopped and admired the sunlight bouncing off her delicate membranes and bright scales, noticing that she wasn't favoring her injured leg. She was truly a magnificent figure.

Thank you, she said, turning to him. *But I didn't ask you out here to give me compliments. I'm worried. I can't find Old Man Winter.*

"Can't find him? What do you mean?"

I can't find him, she repeated, shifting so he could look over her hind leg. *He's not around the cottage, and he's hiding from the scrying pool. That's never good.*

"Did you try and reach him mentally?" Drew asked.

Of course. He's not replying.

Drew leaned against her flank, considering. The pictures from the day before had filled him with hope--maybe the Eidolon's grasp really was weakening. But if Old Man Winter was missing now, and wasn't even responding to Ember..."Has this ever happened before?"

Yes, she said softly, dipping her head. *Usually when he went to gather his wolves.*

As she spoke, a wolf howled in the distance, and a shiver went down Drew's spine. "What does he use his wolves for?"

To hunt. Her voice was hushed. *To kill.*

The wolves howled again, closer, and Drew and Ember exchanged solemn glances. "Have we been wrong?" Drew asked her. "Was it all just an act, to lull us into complacency?"

Eidolons work in mysterious ways, Ember said, looking out towards the hills. *Then again, perhaps I am over-reacting.*

"Maybe." Drew hoped so. "He looked so happy yesterday."

Maybe I'm wrong. Perhaps he just needed some time alone. She sighed. *I wish he would respond.*

It was flurrying again outside--short bursts of tiny snowflakes that lasted maybe fifteen minutes, then gave way to wan sunshine before coming back to fill the air with little white flakes again. Molly and Schrodinger hurried along the street, heading for the downtown area to finish their shopping.

"Okay, so we still need to get Mom's gift, and something for the Yankee swap at the store," Molly said, trying to look at her list and avoid other people at the same time. The sidewalks were full of holiday shoppers and people looking at all the displays. It was hard to believe there were only five days left until Christmas. Where had the month gone?

We also need to pick up the last part of Drew's present, Schrodinger said. *Mick said it would be in today.*

"Right." Molly added another note to her list. "And we need to stop at the grocery store and get the dried cherries for the scones Mom asked me to make for Christmas morning." She sighed. "It's a good thing Jack, Lily, and Kaylee are done already. We wouldn't be able to carry much more!"

We could make two trips, if needed, Schrodinger reminded her. *We have all day, after all.*

"Yes, we do. And if we make two trips, we can have lunch in between."

They hit the grocery store first, since it was on their way, and the cherries wouldn't be hurt by walking around all day. Also, Molly didn't want to have anything like chocolate sneaking into her backpack--she had too much at home already.

After the grocery store, they ducked into the Hammered Dulcimer to pick up the music box that her mother had been lusting over since September. It was a little Irish cottage that played a lovely Irish lullaby, and Mrs. Barrett had remarked how much it looked like the cottage that she and her husband had spent their honeymoon in. Molly had arranged with Russ, the owner, to put it aside for her. The look on her mother's face when they went in the next time and found it gone had been priceless. Molly was looking forward to her unwrapping it on Christmas morning.

The Dulcimer was crowded with people, so Molly didn't stay long. Russ had the jewelry box packaged to go, so she slipped it into her backpack and called out, "Thanks, Russ!" before ducking back out into the snow. He waved and turned back to the next customer in line.

Where now? Schrodinger asked as she rejoined him outside the Dulcimer's window. Russ had set up a village scene with various jewelry boxes nestled in between the buildings. Miniature lights glowed and twinkled, and there was a little train that wound through the town. The CrossCat had opted to stay outside and watch the window, rather than go in and risk getting stepped on.

Molly stared at her list, trying to decide. "Let's go see Catherine next," she said finally. "I need to put in my order for more boxes for the next month, and I want to see what she has for miniature Christmas ornaments."

You mean we don't have enough? There are still 5 days left!

"Not for us, silly cat!" Molly laughed, weaving her way through the crowds, Schrodinger keeping pace with her. "For gifts! I want to get some to tie onto the presents for the Trio and the techs."

Instead of the edible tags?

"No, with them." Molly had started a tradition about five years ago of putting edible tags made with her special sugar cookie dough and royal icing on her best friends' presents. "If I stopped doing the tags, I think there would be a revolt!"

Probably.

They threaded their way up the street to the Tin Shop, which was one of Molly's favorite stores in the Cove. Catherine Taylor not only gathered the best little boxes and bags to put all sorts of stuff in, but she collected local artists and interesting pieces from every Realm she could get a finger into. Molly often wondered how she managed to get some of the things she had. The stock in the store seemed to change daily, and there was always something new to find.

Today, Catherine had eschewed turning on the regular lights in the store. When Molly pushed open the door, she and

Schrodinger entered a world of intertwined Christmas lights. Not flickering, but twined together in such a way that they spread pools of colored light over the inventory.

It was like walking into a rainbow.

"Oh wow," Molly breathed, as she and Schrodinger made their way through the store, passing from color to color. The lights sparkled off beads, glass, silver, and gold, casting amazing shadows on everything. "This is awesome."

Agreed.

They found Catherine at the back of the store, talking to an older woman who was seated at a small table, a tray full of seed beads in front of her. A small brilliant light was attached to the edge of her table, and a wine bottle half-sheathed in a shining bead net glowed in the light the lamp cast.

"Molly! Schrodinger!" Catherine grinned at them. "Merry Christmas! I've been wondering when I'd see you."

"Merry Christmas," Molly said, but her attention was riveted on the bottle. The older woman smiled at her and motioned her closer.

"Ah, so you're Molly," the older woman said, her brown eyes twinkling. "I've looked forward to meeting you. I've heard a lot about you."

Molly blinked. "You have? From who?" Then, as the woman reached into the bag at her feet, she said, "Oh, Drew! But how did he find you? Who are you?"

"We met this past fall, after Catherine put us in touch. My name is Anne Griswold, and I've been doing this for years." Anne held out a small gift bag to Molly. "I was going to stop in your tea shop later today. He and one of his friends were wandering through here and he saw my bottles." She smiled down at Schrodinger. "I've heard about you as well. How is the Librarian doing these days?"

You...you know the Librarian? Schrodinger's eyes went wide.

Really? How?

"We've been friends for a long time," Anne told him. "We traveled together for a bit when I was younger. But I haven't seen her lately. I'll have to remedy that after the new year, I think."

Schrodinger looked stunned.

Molly, however, had opened the bag and pulled out an ornament covered in pale pink beads that shimmered in the lights. "And Drew commissioned you to make these for me?"

Anne nodded. "He asked me what else I could bead, ornaments maybe, and then we got to talking. He said you'd had a bad patch, and he was looking for something to make you smile again. As he told me the story, I must say I agree. It sounds like it was a hard fall."

"It was," Molly said, rolling the ball in her fingers. "But this has definitely helped. Especially now."

"Oh? Did he really get you a live Christmas tree to put them on?"

Molly took a seat on a barrel next to her and told Anne about what Drew had arranged as the craftswoman began to work on the bottle again.

"Of course, it was going to be different," Molly finished. "He didn't count on Old Man Winter kidnapping him."

"You are a fascinating person, Molly," Anne said. "In a fascinating town. I haven't been to Carter's Cove before, but now, I think I shall have to make it a regular stop on my travels."

"I hope you will," Catherine said, rejoining them. "I can definitely sell your bottles, and anything else you care to sell." She grinned at Molly. "Drew showed me the ornaments and helped me get in touch with Anne. That's why she's here."

"How long are you here?" Molly asked Anne.

"Another day or so, then I head to my daughter's house, for Christmas," Anne said. "I've three lovely grandchildren waiting for me and Father Christmas with equal anticipation, or so I've been told."

"Then please, stop in at CrossWinds Books tomorrow and have a cup of tea with me before you leave." Molly got up reluctantly. "But we have other things to do today, and I need to order boxes, Catherine."

"I will," Anne said, and got up as well. She was smaller than Molly had realized, but the warmth in the hug she gave her was genuine. "Be well, Molly. Have a Merry Christmas. And thank you for what you do."

"For what I do?" Molly asked, a little confused.

"Old Man Winter affects everyone. If you can save him, then you have saved us all," Anne said.

✳✱✳

Ember was looking for him again. Old Man Winter ignored her questions and trudged on, his boots crackling in the snow. He could have simply teleported to his destination, but it had felt wrong. He needed to walk.

You hunt?

The question drifted out of the woods that he walked through. They hadn't joined him yet, but he had seen the ghostly grey and white shadows moving through the trees.

Yes. Old Man Winter straightened his back. *Yes, I hunt.*

One of the shadows detached itself from the pack and joined him--a huge grey wolf, with white frosting the tips of his fur. *We hunt with you?*

Always. Old Man Winter laid a fond hand on the great wolf's head. *I wouldn't hunt without you.*

Good. The hunt is always fun.

They strode off through the snow together in silence, needing no more words. Old Man Winter had raised the pack from puppies, and they knew what he wanted.

Sometimes more than he did, he realized.

They crested the hill and he paused, looking down at the buildings clustered together in the valley. There was smoke coming from the chimneys, scenting the air with the smells of wood and food. It was quiet, and he could hear the shuffling of livestock in the barns.

We hunt here? The grey wolf sat on his haunches, his tongue lolling out.

Yes, but not yet. Old Man Winter spread his fingers out, summoning the snow snakes he had left over a week prior.

They came, slow and sleek, with rats in their bellies and the memories of the village in their minds. He listened intently as they twined around him and whispered. The wolf waited, unmoved by the sudden appearance of the long white and blue reptiles.

After they had finished, Old Man Winter considered his options. The Eidolon deep within him counseled carnage, of course, but now that he knew what it was, he found it easier to resist. There were children in that village, and families that were trying to survive a bad harvest and a cold winter. The snakes had overheard the men who had set the trap for Ember lamenting how much they could have gotten for her, how they could have provided for the town for years to come. How their buyer was offering even more if they could find her again.

But they had also overheard most of the village celebrating that the dragon had escaped, and how they had shamed the hunters. They had watched the wives teaching their children how to make what little they had last, and watched the men out trying to find food, or work. There was no real Gate for many miles, and there was little else in the area.

Do we hunt? The grey wolf asked him after a long silence.

Yes, Old Man Winter said. *We hunt. Follow me.* And he started down the hill.

Chapter 21
December 21

Molly looked around the kitchen one last time. "I think everything's all set."

It's not like you haven't written everything down for them anyways, or that they don't have your phone number, Schrodinger observed from his stool. *You'd think you were leaving for a week or more, not just one day.*

"Well, I wanted to make sure I'd covered every possibility," Molly said. "He's being wonderful in covering for me tonight. Especially tonight. I don't know how they convinced Mal, considering it's the night before the Ball."

The Snow Queen's annual Christmas Ball was the most important event of the Christmas season in Carter's Cove, except for Christmas Day, and even that was close. For one night, the final Saturday before Christmas, the entire Cove shut down, and everyone donned their best clothes to dance in a magical ballroom in the middle of a forest clearing. The fact that Mal had agreed to let Luke and Steve leave the Gate Station to cover the tea shop for three hours before Aunt Margie closed the store for the night was nothing short of amazing. Especially since they were already short-handed without Drew.

It's because it's for you, Schrodinger said.

"You make me sound like someone important," Molly told him, pulling out the box of spare mugs from the pantry and putting it on the island. "I'm just me."

You're the one who makes sure everyone is happy and okay, Schrodinger told her. *You're the one who goes out with cookies and baked goods and dinner when someone isn't feeling well. You're the one who is always able to help out with cookies or cupcakes or something at the last minute.*

"Now you're making me sound like a saint," Molly said, laughing a little because she was blushing. "I'm most definitely not. I'm just Molly."

"Never just Molly," Luke said, coming into the kitchen. There was snow in his dark hair and covering his jacket. Steve, coming in behind him, looked frozen and absolutely miserable.

"Just Molly," she said firmly. "Let me get you guys some tea to warm up."

"Bless you," Steve said, shedding his jacket. "I've never been so cold in my life. I have no idea how you guys handle it every year."

"It's been really cold this month," Molly said, pouring hot water into two of her bigger mugs. She set the large tea box in front of them. "Colder than usual."

"That's what people have been telling me," Steve said. "I thought they were just pulling my leg."

She shook her head. "No, I don't remember a December this cold in a long time."

Really? Schrodinger said, and all three of them turned to look at him. *Old Man Winter has been in and out of the Cove on a regular basis this month. Did you think he was just called that for no reason?*

"I didn't even think of that," Luke admitted.

"Me either," Molly said "Well, at least we'll have a white Christmas." She didn't finish the sentence out loud, but she privately wondered if it would be their last Christmas. Had she done enough to break the Eidolon's hold on him?

"Molly?" Luke was looking strangely at her, and for one panicked minute, she wondered if she'd voiced her fears out loud. Then he held up a piece of paper. "You're not expecting us to bake, are you?"

"No." Molly chuckled, and took the recipe that she'd left on top of the note from him. "I need to take that home. There's plenty of goodies in the tins behind you. Here's the tea." And she tapped the dark wooden box. "Aunt Margie said she's closing at six tonight, so you should be all set to run back to the Station." She patted another box on the counter. "Take this back with you. It should salve some of Mal's annoyance."

Both techs' eyes lit up. "Is that..." Luke asked.

She nodded. "Homemade sugar cookies and almond brittle."

"We'll make sure he gets...some," Steve said, and Luke grinned.

"He knows it's coming, so make sure they don't all get eaten," Molly said, and laughed again as their faces fell. "There's plenty in there, I promise!" She shrugged into her coat, and picked up her backpack and her gloves. "I'm going to be home, so feel free to call me if you need anything. DC said she's willing to help too, if you need. Are you all set?"

"Just one thing before you go," Luke said, dipping his hand into his pocket. He pulled out a small white box and handed it to her. "I promised I would get this to you today."

Molly frowned. It was too small to have one of Anne's ornaments in it. "What is it?"

"You can open it and find out," he said.

She opened the box and gasped. Inside, nestled on black velvet, was a glistening crystal snowflake necklace with matching earrings.

"He said he didn't know what color dress you were wearing this year, but figured this would go with everything," Luke said.

"It would," Molly agreed, drawing one finger along the slick surface of the snowflake pendant. "It definitely would."

She and Schrodinger walked out the front door a few minutes later and started to walk down the street towards home. Then they heard, "Ho, Molly!"

As they stopped and turned, Pavel swept up in a small sleigh, pulled by a single bay mare who had silver ribbons braided into her mane. "Would you like a ride?" he asked, grinning at them.

"As long as it's right home," Molly told him. "I don't have time for side trips today. I have a ton of baking to do, and I still have to get ready for tomorrow."

"Just home," Pavel agreed. "I haven't seen you in a couple of days, and to be honest, I missed you."

Molly eyed him, wondering if he was teasing her, but his face was open and honest. Schrodinger had already jumped into the sleigh so after a moment, Molly joined him.

The little sleigh was cozy, with soft seats and a warm woolen blanket that Pavel made sure was tucked around them before he clucked at the horse. She set a sedate pace that kept the wind from freezing their faces.

Are you going to the Ball tomorrow, Pavel? Schrodinger asked.

"I wouldn't miss it," the pirate said. "I hear it's the event of the winter."

"It is," Molly agreed. "Everyone will be there." She paused, then said, "Well, almost everyone."

He'll be there, Molly, Schrodinger said, snuggling up next to her. *He promised he would be!*

"That was before Old Man Winter," Molly said.

Pavel looked at her. "You are doubting your influence? After what happened Wednesday?"

Molly shifted a little under his gaze. "Not doubting so much as worrying," she admitted. "It's hard to believe that just a few cookies and some time together could banish something like an Eidolon. And what if he's just leading me on? He could be preparing to destroy us all along and it's been all for nothing."

"And if he is, that is not your fault," Pavel told her sternly. "You have done your best, Molly. You have reached out to him again and again."

"That will be cold comfort for the people who die," she muttered.

Schrodinger reached out and put a paw on her arm. *I don't think he's going to destroy anything,* he said. *Look at how much fun he had with delivering the gingerbread! You can't fake that!*

Molly thought privately that something like an Eidolon could probably fake anything, but she didn't want to say that, so she smiled at the CrossCat. "I'm sure you're right," she said. "I'm just tired today, that's all."

"Tell me, Miss Molly, why are you leaving work early today?" Pavel asked.

"Because Aunt Margie is afraid I'm getting sick with all the running around with Old Man Winter I've been doing. and so she asked if I could find someone to cover for me," Molly said. "She said she would close the tea room if necessary, but I was to go home and relax."

She's also been working too hard, Schrodinger told Pavel. *Aunt Margie actually told her to sleep, but she won't.*

"It's not a bad idea," Pavel said. "And then you can party more tomorrow."

He dropped them off at their doorstop, waiting until Molly collected the mail and opened the front door. Then he waved and drove off.

There were letters and a small box, and she shuffled through them as she mounted the stairs. The box intrigued her--there was no return address, and no postmark. Someone had dropped it off in her box.

Once they were inside and coats had been shed, she opened the box, with Schrodinger watching. Lying cushioned in dark green cotton was a little black and silver ornament. Rather than a note in Drew's lovely calligraphy, there was a single white flower, somehow uncrushed, looking as if a florist had just cut it from the plant. When Molly picked it up, the sweet scent flooded the apartment, icy and floral at the same time.

What kind of flower is that? Schrodinger asked.

"I don't know," Molly said, examining it. It was cool to the touch, and scented her fingers. "But it's lovely."

Do you think it was Old Man Winter? Or maybe the Snow Queen? What does it mean?

"I don't know," she repeated. "I just don't know."

Drew pulled the scarf up around his mouth to keep the icy wind from sucking the very air from his lungs and plunged out into the snowstorm. He could barely see in front of him, but he had to make sure Ember was okay in the stable. She had assured him she was fine, but he felt the need to see for himself. Luckily, the courtyard wasn't that big, and he could see the vague outline of the stables when the wind shifted.

After several minutes of straining against the wind and snow, he stumbled into the stable doors and managed to get himself inside. The wind howled, as if robbed of a victim, but the stable was blessedly calm.

You didn't have to come out, Ember said to him, poking her head up over the stall door as he shook off snow. *This stable is very solid. We would have been fine.*

"We?" Drew asked, and then looked down the middle of the stable. Four horses poked their heads over the stall doors, looking back at him with mild curiosity. "Where did they come from?"

Old Man Winter brought them in just before the storm hit, Ember said.

"Well, it's a good thing that I came out then," Drew said. "They look okay now, but I think they'd go insane and hurt themselves if you tried to fill their water buckets."

Perhaps. You're a good man, Drew. The dragon watched as he refilled the water buckets and made sure each horse had plenty of hay and a small bit of grain. *I think they would have been fine, though.*

"Depends on how long the storm lasts," Drew said. "I'd rather not have to go out more than once. It's brutal out there." Then he turned to look at her. "Old Man Winter brought them in?"

Yes.

"Did he say where he got them?" Drew ran a hand over the soft nose of the horse in front of him, a small grey mare that blew gently into his hair and then tried to chew on his hat. He moved out of the way and she went back to her hay.

No. He didn't.

Drew thought about that for a few minutes as he finished tidying up the stable. "Well, he hasn't come into the cottage," he said finally. "Maybe he'll be back in a bit and we can ask him then."

"Or maybe he could just tell you now."

Drew turned as Old Man Winter stepped out of the tack room, smoke from his long pipe hanging lazily in the still air. It was amazing, really, how the air in the stable was so peaceful, in contrast to the howling outside.

"Maybe he could," Drew said, folding his arms across his chest. "Where did they come from?"

"Found them wandering out in the snow," Old Man Winter said. "Thought they might like a warm bed on a night like tonight."

"Wandering? Did they have any tack or anything?"

"Nope."

Drew turned back to look more closely at the horses, wondering who was missing them. They were obviously tamed. "I wonder where they came from."

Old Man Winter shrugged, but didn't answer.

How long will the snow last? Ember asked.

"Should blow over by morning," Old Man Winter said.

"That's good to know," Drew said. "They should be fine until then."

"Thought you might like to know, since you'll be leaving once it does," Old Man Winter said, and turned back to the tack room.

"Wait, what?" Drew looked up. "What did you just say?"

"Clean the snow out of your ears," Old Man Winter said acidly. "You're leaving tomorrow. You might want to pack."

"I thought I was going to stay here until you made a decision about the Cove and what you were going to do," Drew said, feeling hope rise in his chest. "Have you made a decision then?"

"About that? No. But I know you made a promise to Molly to take her to the Snow Queen's Ball, and I'm not going to be the reason you break a second promise to her. So get dressed for the party tomorrow." And with that, Old Man Winter walked through the tack room wall and vanished.

Well, that was interesting, Ember said.

"That's one word for it," Drew said, but he couldn't stop the joy that was coursing through him. He wouldn't miss the ball. "Of course, he didn't stay long enough to tell me if he delivered Molly's ornament today."

If he was supposed to, I'm sure he did.

Then Drew thought of something else. "Dammit."

What?

"I don't have time to order Molly a corsage," he said.

Ember chuckled. *Isn't that why you have a pirate friend?*

Chapter 22
December 22

Molly smoothed the front of her dress and picked up her evening bag. Turning to Schrodinger, she said, "Well, what do you think?"

I think you look beautiful, Schrodinger said. *Drew won't be able to keep his eyes off of you.*

"If he's there, you mean." But she smiled and turned back to the mirror one last time. This year, she'd chosen a slim sheath dress of dark blue that ended just above her knees, and dark blue shoes. The dress curved up over her right shoulder and flowed down to her wrist, leaving the other shoulder and arm bare. Drew's snowflakes hung from her ears and nestled between her breasts, glittering in the lights of the mini Christmas tree on the table. She and the Trio had gone out that morning to have their hair and nails done; the result was a sleek up-do that piled curls up on her head, with crystal pins holding it in place.

There was a beep from the street; Molly leaned over and peeked out the window. Lai's Range Rover was parked out in front of the building. "Lai's here!" she said, dropping the curtain. "Are you ready?"

Yes. Don't forget your coat. Schrodinger swiped a final paw across his whiskers and jumped down. Molly had to admit that he looked very dapper in his dark blue bow tie and the dress vest

Sue had found for him.

"Hardly. This dress is pretty but not very warm." Molly went to the bedroom. "Luckily, Aunt Margie let me borrow her mink."

The full-length fur coat fit her perfectly, just like her aunt had promised. Feeling a bit like an old-time movie star, Molly hurried down the stairs, Schrodinger on her heels.

"Wow, you look fabulous!" Lai said, as they slid into the car. "Where did you get that coat?"

"It's Aunt Margie's, and if I get anything on it, I'll be killed," Molly said, clicking her seat belt into place. "So no, you can't make it accidentally disappear."

"Darn." Lai chuckled. "Ah well." She looked in the rear-view mirror. "You all set back there?"

Ready to go!

"Then we're off!" Lai threw the Rover into gear and they headed out into the snow.

There was a line of cars headed out to the Snow Queen's Ball-- Lai fell in behind a large limo. "You ready for this?" she asked.

"Of course." Molly flipped down the mirror and checked her makeup one last time.

"Do you think Drew will be there?" Lai glanced at her. "Have you heard anything?"

Molly shook her head.

"Well, we can hope," Lai said, and that was that.

They didn't talk any more until they reached the clearing. Lai stopped by the valet, and they stepped out into the night air.

Schrodinger jumped down from the car and then sniffed. *Do you smell that?*

"Smell what?" Molly sniffed the air.

It's snow.

"It's winter," Lai said. "And it's been snowing on and off for the last two days."

No, it doesn't smell like that, Schrodinger said. He looked up at

Molly. *This smells like him.*

"Old Man Winter?" she said.

Yes.

Excitement sluiced through her. Surely he wouldn't show up without Drew. "Then let's go!" Molly hurried towards the clearing as fast as her heels would allow her, with Schrodinger and Lai right behind her.

They dropped off their coats with the coat check, then entered the main ball room. As always, it was like entering a winter fantasy world, one where the snow fell but the air temperature was that of a warm spring day. Molly looked around, hoping to spot either Drew or Old Man Winter.

She didn't see either of them, but she did see Jade already on her throne, watching the dancers with a smile on her lovely face. Her dress was long, edged with pale blue and silver, and her tiara was stylized snowflakes that held her long hair away from her brow. Jade waved to them and then turned to say something to one of the people standing around her throne.

"Can you find them?" Molly asked Schrodinger.

If I can't, I'll turn in my CrossCat card. He was off before he'd finished the sentence.

"Come on," Lai said, taking Molly's arm. "Let's go find Noemi and Sue."

✳✴✳

"Come ON, boy! I swear, you take longer than a woman to get ready!"

Drew rolled his eyes and finished tying his tie. "I'm almost ready."

"The ball will be over before we even get there!" Old Man Winter snapped, pacing up and down the bedroom Drew had lived in for most of the month.

"Hardly." Drew ran his hands through his hair once more,

and then grabbed his bag. Funny how little he actually had with him. "All right," he said. "I'm ready."

"About time," Old Man Winter grumbled.

"Hey, I haven't seen Molly in a month!" Drew said. "You can't blame me for wanting to look good for her. Besides," and he gave the old man a long look, "I see you took some pains in how you look too."

"And it didn't take me three hours." Old Man Winter took a hold of Drew's arm. "Hold still."

Snow swirled around them, blinding Drew momentarily. When he was able to see again, he realized two things.

One was that he was warm again. Almost too warm.

The second was that he was surrounded by people.

The music faltered and died as he blinked, straightening up a bit. Old Man Winter had simply teleported them into the center of the Snow Queen's ball room, and everyone had taken a few steps back, probably unnerved by their sudden appearance.

Molly and Lai stood together by a pillar, both of them looking at him, eyes wide and mouths open. The dark blue satin dress hugged every curve of her body, and the blue heels added inches to her height. She looked sleek, sophisticated, and utterly perfect. He dropped his bag and pushed through the frozen crowd to her.

Folks melted out of the way: all Drew could see was Molly, standing in a pool of white light, snowflakes sparkling in her ears and around her neck. Then she was in his arms and her lips met his.

"You made it," she whispered once the kiss broke, her eyes bright.

"I promised I would," he said, and kissed her again.

Then she pulled back, fear on her face. "Are you leaving again?"

"No." Drew hugged her close, resting his chin on the top of her head, feeling the soft curls against his skin. "No, I'm home to stay."

✳✳✳

Old Man Winter watched them, and his heart ached, as much from the howl of rage in his head as from the scene in front of him. There was love in the very air around Molly and Drew, and it was clear that they didn't care who saw it. He hadn't seen love like that in a very long time.

He turned away, and went over to the Snow Queen, who was watching him with a knowing smile on her face. "Hello, Old Man," she said. "You always did like to make an entrance."

"Jade," he said gruffly. "You're looking well."

"So are you." She looked at his dark grey suit and tie with approval. "I'd forgotten how well you clean up when you care to."

He grunted. "Mind if I join you?"

"Not at all." She waved a hand, and one of her footmen brought a chair out to set beside her icy throne.

From the dais, Old Man Winter had a good view of the entire room. Molly and Drew had withdrawn to a table with friends, and Schrodinger was sitting some tables away from them with three other CrossCats, one of whom he recognized. "You have a lot of interesting people here this year," he said, gesturing with his beard at the Librarian. "Haven't seen her out of her den in years."

"Schrodinger is her grandson," Jade said. "She wanted to see where and why he stopped his wanderings."

"I thought he was young."

"He is," she agreed. "But I think he's found his home. He's one of the lucky ones who didn't have to wander far." She hesitated, then switched to mental speech so she wouldn't disrupt the others around her. *The question is, will it still be here after Christmas Day?*

The question hurt him, and he avoided looking at her. *I don't want to talk about it today. Let me enjoy the party with everyone else.* "If I could eat Molly's cooking every day, I'm not sure I would leave either."

It's been a long time since I've heard you say that. "I'm sure she'd be happy to supply you. I've never had any issues with ordering things from the Cove."

Old Man Winter was about to say something else when one of the footmen leaned forward and murmured something in Jade's ear, too low for him to hear.

"Of course he can," Jade said. "He shouldn't have to ask." As the footman went off through the crowd, she turned to Old Man Winter. "Although it doesn't surprise me. You aren't the only one who likes to make an entrance."

He raised an eyebrow at her.

There was a stir at the back of the room then, and everyone turned again. Old Man Winter sighed and Jade hid a grin behind her hand as Pavel swept into the room.

"He has no idea how to be subtle, does he?" Old Man Winter said.

"He does, when he wants to," Jade said. "He doesn't always want to."

Pavel swaggered up to the throne, dressed in tight black pants that looked like he'd painted them on, thigh-high leather boots that shone in the light, and a white shirt that gushed lace from the throat and cuffs. Gold glinted in his ear, and his coat was a dark maroon brocade that Old Man Winter noticed had skulls and snowflakes woven into it. "My lady Snow Queen, how lovely to see you," he said, pulling off his hat and sweeping her an elaborate bow, the white feather plume swishing through the air. "It has been too long."

"Indeed, my lord Captain, I have sorely missed your company," Jade said, her lips twitching but her tone solemn. "I think it deplorable that you have deprived me of it."

"Twas not my aim, Your Grace," he assured her. "I have been busy."

"Too busy to spare me a visit?" One pale eyebrow rose. "Do I mean that little to you then?"

Old Man Winter coughed to cover the laughter that rose up in his throat at the look of dismay on Pavel's face.

"Of course not, Your Excellency! I have been traveling to find the right gifts for you, so as to not show up empty-handed!" The pirate replaced the hat on his head and reached into his coat, drawing a silken bag from a hidden pocket. "May I?"

"I await your tribute with bated breath," she said, and gestured. Her footmen brought out a small table, and Pavel emptied the bag onto it.

"Will this suffice?" he asked.

The pouch disgorged a stream of silver and golden snowflakes, glittering in the light. Jade got up and went down to run her fingers through them, her dress whispering in the silence.

"It will, for the moment," she said, and then smiled at him warmly. "I have missed you."

"And I you."

She embraced him then. "You are a scoundrel," she said. "And I assume you have something else to do here, Captain?"

"I do." He nodded. "Have I permission to discharge my duty?"

"You do." Jade tried to level a stern gaze at him, and he winked at her. "But don't forget who holds your letter of marque, Captain Chekhov. I expect to see you more than once every few years."

"Your servant, My Queen." Pavel winked and bowed again, then turned, looking for Molly. He went over to her and Drew and pulled out a small corsage box.

"You never told me you held his letter of marque," Old Man Winter said, as Jade returned to her throne, a silver snowflake in her hands.

"I don't tell you a lot of things, Old Man," she said, and gave him a mysterious smile. "It's more fun that way."

Old Man Winter grunted and watched as Molly removed the corsage. The day's ornament dangled from it, as he had thought.

This little ball was sliver, with a myriad of rainbow beads at the intersections.

"He sent one to her every day in December," he said.

"He loves her very much," Jade replied. "You should ask him about what he did last year."

"You shouldn't have used her, you know," he said then.

"You shouldn't have forced my hand."

There wasn't much he could say to that.

Chapter 23
December 23

Molly yawned and considered snuggling back into sleep for a bit longer. Aunt Margie was opening late as she always did after the Snow Queen's Ball, so she had time. All in all, spending the morning in bed with her two favorite boys sounded like a perfectly splendid way to start her day.

She rolled over to see if Drew was awake yet. Schrodinger was still sleeping, a warm lump by her feet, but the other half of the bed, which she'd been sure had been occupied last night...was empty.

Did I dream it all? Molly thought, stretching out a hand. The sheets were cool to the touch. *Was it all just a dream, and he's still with Old Man Winter?*

And then the smell of frying bacon wafted through the room and she sighed in relief. *Not a dream.*

Schrodinger's eyes half-opened as the bacon smell hit his nostrils. *Breakfast?*

"It certainly smells like it, but we can save you some if you want."

His eyes closed again, and he snuggled back down into the nest he'd made in the blankets at the foot of the bed. Molly laughed and got up, shivering a little as her feet hit the wooden floor. Once again, she put "getting a rug for the bedroom" on her mental list.

Drew looked up from the stove when she came into the kitchen. "Morning, beautiful," he said, as if he hadn't been gone nearly a month. "Tea's ready."

"There is nothing sexier than a guy cooking bacon in a tee-shirt and pajama pants," Molly said, coming up behind him and giving him a hug before she made a beeline for the coffee pot that she used to make tea. He'd loaded the top with her favorite Christmas tea, and she poured cups for both of them as he transferred the crisp bacon to a pan that he slipped into the warm oven.

"It feels odd to be the one sitting and watching you cook," Molly said, taking a seat at the table. "Nice, but odd."

Drew laughed as he broke eggs into the bacon grease. "I was a little worried about this, to be honest. Not sure how my plebeian efforts will stand up to your kitchen witch standards."

"Bacon and eggs sound heavenly," Molly assured him. "And there are muffins in the fridge, if you want."

"Already warming in the oven."

"And you were worried?" Molly laughed a little. "You have everything under control."

"You haven't tasted it yet," he warned her, and then looked around. "No Schrodinger?"

"I told him we'd save him some. He's still sleeping."

Schrodinger had danced the night away at the Ball, thrilled beyond belief at Drew's reappearance and the fact that there had been three other CrossCats there, not the least of which had been the Librarian. Molly and Drew had barely seen him most of the night, catching random glimpses of him through the crowd. He'd been so tired that he'd fallen asleep on the ride home and hadn't even stirred when Drew carried him up from Lai's car, or when Molly had undressed him and put him on the bed.

"He was very excited last night about those other CrossCats," Drew said. "Especially the big black one."

"That's the Librarian, his teacher." Molly blew on her tea to cool it a little. "And his grandmother. He worships her."

"Ah."

The kitchen grew silent as Drew concentrated on his eggs and Molly sipped her tea, enjoying the homey feel of the morning. It was still snowing out, she realized, after taking a peek out the dining nook window: a light, fluffy snow that muffled everything and left the world enveloped in peace and cold.

"What are your plans today?" she asked, as he slid a plate of fried eggs, crispy bacon, and cranberry-orange muffins dripping butter towards her.

"I've got shopping to do," he said, putting his own plate down across from her. "And I might see if Schrodinger wants to come with me."

"He might."

He might what?

Molly and Drew turned to see Schrodinger stumble into the kitchen, his eyes still half-closed. "You could have slept more," Molly said, getting up to get his normal morning cup of Earl Grey. "We don't have to be into work until noon, and it's barely nine o'clock."

Hungry. Schrodinger didn't even try to jump up on to his chair; he just stood next to it, leaning against it for stability. Molly tried to suppress a giggle.

"Well, here, eat this and then you can go back to bed," she said, putting his tea and the plate that Drew handed her in front of him. "Drew wanted to know if you wanted to spend time with him today. He needs help shopping."

'Kay. Schrodinger made it through about half the plate and all of his tea before he turned and shambled back to bed.

"Think he made it onto the bed?" Drew asked Molly as they finished eating.

"I'll be surprised if he made it out of the living room, to be honest," she said.

They found him snuggled under the Christmas tree in the living room, fast asleep, his head on one of his stuffed toys. Molly ran for her phone--it was too cute a picture to pass up. Then she and Drew curled up on the couch together for a bit and enjoyed a second cup of tea while he told her everything that had happened over the past month.

"Do you really think we did it?" Molly asked, leaning her head back against his chest. "Do you think we defeated the Eidolon?"

"I don't know," Drew said. "He's a very deep, complex person, and Ember said the Eidolon has had a very long time to work on him. But he seemed to have fun last night. And he brought me back."

"Maybe that's the sign we did succeed," Molly said.

"Maybe." But she heard the doubt in his voice.

Later that morning, Drew and Schrodinger walked with her as far as CrossWinds Books, then turned to walk to the downtown area to shop. Molly, unsure as to what she would find in her kitchen, had come in an hour early, just to give herself time to clean up anything the boys might have left behind on Friday night, and to start baking. The store was quiet and still, just the way she liked it.

She needn't have worried about a mess. The kitchen was spotless, as was the tea room, and there was a fire ready to be kindled in the wood stove. She dropped her stuff in its customary corner of the kitchen, then went out to start the fire. Once it was burning merrily, she went back into the kitchen...

And stopped. Sitting on one of the stools was Old Man Winter.

"Good morning," she said after a few moments. "I wasn't expecting to see you today."

He grunted. "Wanted to see you before anyone else came in. Hard to talk to you when you're working."

"It can get busy in here," Molly agreed, going over to the stove and turning the kettle on. "Would you like a cup of tea?"

"Yes, please. Some of your Christmas tea, I think."

She pulled out two mugs from the dishwasher, and dropped tea bags into them. Then she went into the pantry and found a box of orange scones.

"Did you have a good time last night?' Molly asked him, as she brought the scones out.

"Yes," Old Man Winter said, and his eyes lit up at the box. "You looked very pretty."

She dimpled. "Thank you!" And then she became serious. "And thank you for bringing Drew back home. It means a lot to me and Schrodinger."

"Didn't seem right to keep him away any longer." Old Man Winter hesitated a minute, and then said, "I'm sorry, Molly."

"For what?"

"For ruining your December." He scowled down at the scone in his hand. "I didn't realize that Jade would drag you into our dispute."

"She was worried about you," Molly said. "And if I can help save you, I will."

"Doesn't it ever get tiring, saving people?" he asked her, looking up. The darkness in his eyes was bottomless. "Don't you ever just want to give up?"

"Sometimes," she admitted quietly. "And sometimes there are people I can't save. But I won't know until I try." She reached out to him, laying a hand on his arm. "Have I saved you?"

He didn't answer for a long time, and ice started to creep through her veins. "I don't know," he said finally. "I'll know by Christmas Day."

"Why Christmas Day?"

"Because if the Eidolon wants to take me completely, it will do it that night," he said. "Just at the break of dawn."

"Can I do anything to help you fight it?" she said.

The ghost of a smile pulled at his lips. "You already have, my dear. But there's one more thing I need to do. And I have to do it alone." He stood up and then he pulled a small ornament out of his pocket. "Drew let me give you today's."

Molly looked at the little green and white ornament, and then pressed it back into his hand. "You keep it," she said, folding his fingers over it. "To remember us by."

✳✳✳

Drew quickly realized that shopping was going to take him a lot longer than it normally would have. Everyone wanted to come up and talk to him on the street, and it wasn't for just quick chats. He and Schrodinger finally ducked into the coffee shop, as much to escape the questions as to pick up the gift Mick had ordered for him.

"Welcome home," Katarina said, drying her hands on her apron and coming out to give him a hug. "We were thrilled to hear you were back."

Drew hugged her warmly. "I missed you all."

"Mick's in the back," she said, gesturing with her head as she knelt to give Schrodinger a hug too. "Why don't you go join him?"

The back of the coffee shop was redolent with the rich smells of chocolate and coffee, and Drew paused to inhale as he stepped into the kitchen. Mick greeted him with a warm hug as well, then nodded towards a stool as he went back to grinding coffee beans.

"Fancy a cup?" he said.

"Love one." Drew accepted the steaming hot coffee, laced with some of Mick's special Scotch, and sighed.

"Heavy sigh," the Scotsman observed. "Did you come for it?"

Drew sipped the coffee and sighed again, this time in happiness. "I've missed this. So it came in then?"

"Of course it did." Mick sounded slightly offended. "Came in yesterday."

He cleaned his hands off and then went into the other part of the kitchen. When he came back, he had a small box in his hands that he gave to Drew.

Drew set his coffee cup aside and opened the box. Inside were two custom cookie molds, both with CrossCats curled up on them. Katarina had shown him a picture of similar molds two months ago, molds that her uncle in Vienna was carving, and he'd put in an order. On one, the CrossCat was surrounded by books, and was reading from a huge tome. On the other, the CrossCat was curled up with a cup of tea and a scone, while cookies fell like raindrops behind him.

"I can't believe he made these," Drew said, touching one of the molds. "They're amazing." He replaced them in the box and said, "And the other piece?"

"Right here." Mick handed him a small bottle of vanilla liquor that he imported from his cousin in the islands. Molly adored baking with it.

"Thanks, man." Drew put the precious bottle into his messenger bag along with the molds.

Schrodinger looked up at him. *What about her ornament for today?*

"Old Man Winter asked if he could deliver one more to her yesterday before we left," Drew said. "So I gave him today's, since Pavel already had yesterday's."

Do you think we did it? Schrodinger said.

"I hope so," Drew said, picking up his coffee cup. "I hope so."

Me too.

Chapter 24
December 24

"Do you see her yet?"

Not yet, but I'm not surprised, Schrodinger said. *Lai said they were going to go out for a Christmas Eve drink after work.* The CrossCat came back into the living room and looked at Drew. *How much more time do you need?*

Drew taped down the last flap on the box he was wrapping. "Done!" he said, and slid the box under the tree. "Now all we have to do is wrap the stuff for the kids and Jack, because I'm sure she's done with mine."

Really? Schrodinger winked at him. *I don't know, she mentioned something about a coal deposit she had to hit...* Then he ducked out of the way as Drew threw a bow at him.

"Must be for you, Cat!" Drew said, chuckling. "I haven't done anything to deserve coal!"

Schrodinger batted the bow back at him and Drew ducked, then threw another bow, and the fight was on. By the time Molly opened the front door and came into the living room from the kitchen, there were shreds of ribbon and paper balls all over the floor, and tinsel hung in the air like confetti.

"What is going on?" she asked, her hands on her hips and a stern expression on her face. Drew and Schrodinger froze in mid-tussle, staring up at her in guilty horror.

Drew had pieces of tinsel and ribbon hanging from his hair; he had a death grip on an empty tube of wrapping paper and there was tape stuck to his sweater. Schrodinger's teeth were sunk into the other end of the tube, a huge bow was stuck to his back, and one of his paws had a box around it.

Molly looked at them, and at the room, which was awash with glitter, pieces of paper, and tinsel, and then looked back at them. Both Drew and Schrodinger waited for the explosion. *At least we didn't hit the tree,* Drew thought, as she continued to look around.

"Hi," he said finally, when the silence had stretched too long. "Um, we were just...cleaning up." He dropped his end of the wrapping tube. "Right, Schrodinger?"

Uh, right! The CrossCat dropped the tube as well, and hurriedly kicked the box off his paw.

"Of course you were." Molly looked around the room and then at the bag in her hands. "I'll just go put this away while you do."

Drew and Schrodinger exchanged looks as she retreated to the kitchen. They heard the refrigerator door open, then close, and then the giggling started. They both breathed a sigh of relief.

"Let's get this cleaned up," Drew said, grabbing the trash can beside the couch. Schrodinger put the much-damaged cardboard tube into the trash and then helped pick up the debris. By the time Molly came back in with a couple of filled wine glasses, the living room had been restored to some semblance of normality.

"At least you didn't hit the tree," she noted, handing one glass to Drew.

"No, we were trying to be careful." Drew showed the glass to Schrodinger, who sniffed and then wrinkled his nose.

Ick, the CrossCat said. *How can you drink that stuff?*

"Same way you and Jack drink out of the horse troughs when we visit the stable," Molly said, settling down on the floor in front of the Christmas tree. "Did you guys at least get everything wrapped before you decided to fight?"

"We just have the stuff for Lily, Kaylee, and Jack to go," Drew said, joining her. "That's it."

It was a quiet way to spend an evening--Drew was an only child, and his cousins had all been older (and male, come to think of it), so he'd never shopped for little girls before. Molly had gotten plenty of things for all three of them, and the pile of wrapped presents grew steadily until the tree was nearly swamped underneath them.

"Just one question," Drew said, when they were finally finished and back up on the couch.

"Mmm?" Molly asked, settling back against him.

"How are we getting all this stuff to your parents' house?"

She giggled. "Nathan's coming by in a bit to pick them all up while Lily helps Mom decorate cookies. We just have to get ourselves over there tomorrow, and I figured we could take the snowmobile over."

"Works for me."

They sat there in the glow of the Christmas tree, sipping wine and listening to WCOV replay the King's College choral from earlier in the day. Schrodinger was sleeping in his bed near the tree.

Nathan showed up about ten o'clock to get the presents, and Molly and Drew helped him carry them down to the car. "Be careful driving home," Molly told him. "This snow is pretty thick."

"Don't worry, I'll go slow," her younger brother promised. "I'll text you when I get home."

They watched him drive off, and then went back upstairs. Molly was yawning, but insisted on staying up until Nathan texted.

"Well, here," Drew said, handing her a small wrapped box. "You might as well open this while we're waiting."

She smiled at him. "The last ornament?"

"I couldn't miss Christmas Eve, could I?" he replied, as she opened it. The ornament was a wine-dark crimson, with gold beads at the intersections.

"This was amazing," Molly said, after she'd hung it on the little tree on the dining room table. The tree glowed with all the ornaments. "Thank you."

"No, thank you," Drew said. "I couldn't have gotten through this year without you."

"That's supposed to be my line, isn't it?" Molly teased him, and he kissed the tip of her nose.

"It's true, though," Drew said, and then gave her a real kiss.

The buzzing of her phone broke them apart. "Nathan must have made it home," Molly said, picking up the pone from the table and looking at it. "That was fast."

"Too fast," Drew said, craning his head to look at the screen. "That's not from Nathan."

"No."

The message was from a number he didn't recognize, and from the furrow in her brow, Molly didn't recognize it either. She clicked on the message and it popped up.

"Get Schrodinger and Drew, dress warmly, and come outside."

They exchanged looks. "Who could it be?" Molly asked.

"I don't know, but I have an idea," Drew said, reaching for his coat. "Let's go find out."

Molly roused Schrodinger and together the three of them went down to the street. Nothing but white snowflakes greeted them. The entire street was empty--between the snow and the fact that it was late on Christmas Eve, everyone else had retired to their warm homes.

Drew was about to suggest that it must have been a prank, and that they should go back in, when Schrodinger stiffened. "What do you see?" Drew asked the CrossCat.

Bells! I hear bells! Like before!

And then out of the snow came the massive reindeer, bells ringing as they pulled Old Man Winter and his giant sledge along. They came right up to the trio and Old Man Winter, wrapped in his furs like the first time Drew had seen him, looked down at them.

"Don't just stand there," he growled. "Get in. We have unfinished business."

Chapter 25
December 25

The reindeer leapt forward through the endless snow, seemingly tireless. Molly, Drew, and Schrodinger were snuggled under a mountain of fur, protected from the wind. Old Man Winter stood behind them, not seeming to mind the cold. Drew and Schrodinger had succumbed to sleep at some point during the long ride, but Molly couldn't, despite her fatigue. She simply sat, warm in the pile of furs, watching the snowy terrain slide by.

They had been traveling for hours. Realms flashed by them; she was certain they had gone on and off several different Roads, and where they would end up, only Old Man Winter knew. She wondered if he were still trying to make his decision. Or if he wanted them there for some other reason.

The sledge shifted on the snow, and she slid down a bit deeper into the furs, ending up lying on her back. Above her, the sky was dark and clear, despite the snowflakes swirling around them. Stars sparkled, brilliant fireflies of ice and light against a black velvet backdrop, but not in any configuration she recognized. Would she ever see the familiar stars above the Cove again? Would the Cove even exist after the dawn? Would she?

Her eyes slowly closed, fatigue finally winning against fear. Molly fell into darkness, lulled to sleep by the hissing of the sledge through the snow.

It was the absence of that hissing that woke her. The sledge had finally come to a halt, and she realized blearily that Old Man Winter was gone. Molly struggled to sit up, trying to shake the cotton wool from her head and see where he was.

She was almost free of the furs when she saw him. The eastern sky was beginning to shade from black to dark blue; soon the sun would be coming up in rose and gold flames over the snow. Old Man Winter stood at the edge of a cliff, looking out and down at something. Molly slipped from the sledge, being careful not to wake Drew or Schrodinger, and joined him.

"Merry Christmas," she said quietly when he turned to look at her. He didn't say anything, but nodded once and turned back to whatever he'd been watching.

She followed his gaze and saw the entire Cove laid out before her, still sleeping in the predawn. The Christmas lights, normally turned off during the darkest hours of the night, had been left on for Christmas Eve, and the Cove sparkled with brilliant pools of color.

Still Old Man Winter said nothing, so Molly watched with him in silence as the sun crept over the horizon, watched the stars dim and blink out, one by one. Drew joined her, and then Schrodinger, and still no one spoke. The four of them watched the sun rise over Carter's Cove, and Molly wondered if it was for the last time.

"Well?" Drew said finally, as the last star winked out. "Are you going to do it?"

"Do what?" Old Man Winter asked irritably, as if annoyed that Drew had broken the silence.

Are you going to destroy the Cove? Schrodinger asked quietly.

A wolf howled in the distance, and was joined by other howls, a chorus that wrapped around them and chilled Molly more than the wind had.

"Are you?" she asked, reaching out her hand. "Has the

Eidolon won?"

Then, finally, Old Man Winter turned to them, and to Molly's surprise, there were tears in his eyes, and a soft smile on his face.

"Yes," he said, and her heart sank. "The Eidolon has won." Then he added, "But not the one you think did."

They blinked at him.

"There are Eidolons of good things as well as evil, Molly, and they work through all sorts of people," he said. "You reminded me of the good in life, and the good in people. Jade was right--the Cove needs to be protected, and you three are the best protectors they could have."

He held his hands out before him and snow danced out from his palms, swirling around him. "I can only add my blessing to it," Old Man Winter said, and released the snow to settle over the Cove, a fine dusting of sugar sparkling in the light of the rising sun. Then Old Man Winter turned and led them back to the sledge. "Come, I'll take you home."

We're going to the farmhouse, Schrodinger said.

"Then I'll take you there."

The ride back to Molly's parents' house was quiet, but unlike the prior ride, the mood was full of joy, not despair. Molly leaned against Drew and snuggled Schrodinger in her lap, letting the wind blow her sleepiness away. There would be time for sleep later.

As they drew up to the house, Molly wondered if anyone was awake yet. It was early, but not early enough for Jack not to notice the reindeer. He tore out of the house, baying joyfully, and Lily, rubbing sleep from her eyes, followed.

She saw the reindeer and her little eyes widened. "Santa?"

"Not quite," Molly said, letting Schrodinger jump out and run over to her. "But I think he knows him."

"Molly? Drew?" Lily looked absolutely confused. "Schrodinger? Why are you riding in there?"

Old Man Winter gave us a ride! Schrodinger told her. *It was awesome!*

"Do the reindeer fly?" she asked.

"They can," Old Man Winter said, laughing a little. "Perhaps some time I shall take you. But now, I have other things to do. And it's time for you to open presents, isn't it?"

Lily nodded, and she, Jack, and Schrodinger ran into the house. Drew followed them, but as Molly got off the sledge, Old Man Winter put a hand on her shoulder. Surprised, she turned back to him.

"Merry Christmas, Molly," he said, and held out his hand. Snowflakes danced and spun over his open palm, and as she watched, it coalesced into a glass globe. Within the glass, she saw a miniature version of the Cove, Christmas lights glimmering and snow glittering. He handed the globe to her and smiled.

"Merry Christmas, Old Man Winter," she said, and stepped back from the sledge, cradling the globe in her hands. "Don't be a stranger."

"I won't. Drew knows where to find me. And so does Jade."

The reindeer reared and took off in a spray of white. Molly stood and watched until they were out of sight. And then she went into the house, stepping into the warmth of her family, and relaxed.

It was Christmas, and life was good.

About the Author

Val Griswold-Ford is the author of the Dark Horseman novels *Not Your Father's Horseman*, *Dark Moon Seasons* and *Last Rites*, all from Dragon Moon Press. She is the co-editor (with Tee Morris) of the memorial anthology *Tales of the Tesla Ranger*. She is also the co-editor of *The Complete Guide to Writing Fantasy: the Opus Magnus* (with Tee Morris) and *The Complete Guide to Writing Fantasy: The Author's Grimoire* (with Lai Zhao), also from Dragon Moon Press, and has self-published the short e-novella *Snow* and, most recently, the short story *Convoy*. She has published several short stories in various anthologies online and in print, and is owned by three cats. She lives in New Hampshire with said cats.

You can find her at www.vg-ford.com or on Twitter as @vg_ford. Her Patreon website is https://www.patreon.com/vgford, where she is releasing new fiction on a regular basis.

www.ingramcontent.com/pod-product-compliance
Lightning Source LLC
Chambersburg PA
CBHW061142170626
46809CB00003B/960